Th

Forbid

Tattie Maggard

PLEASE NOTE: This is a Swiss Amish series (not Pennsylvania Dutch) consisting of three parts: The Broken, The Forbidden, and The Secret. They must be read in order.

Chapter 1

Emily seemed to only blink her eyes and it was winter once again, the school-break for Christmas, a welcome vacation. She'd thrown herself into her work this school year and accomplished much, not only with the students at school, but in remaining pure in her thoughts.

Silas sat at her kitchen table sipping coffee with his hat on, no doubt still trying to warm himself from the bitter cold of morning chores. He was handsome as ever, but Emily tried to view him like the decorations in the buildings in Asheville—to be enjoyed occasionally, and from a distance.

It was Christmas Eve, and Emily debated if she should give Silas the gift basket she made for him or not. She knew the gift was too personal for friends. Would he tell anyone about it, giving them the wrong idea? She certainly couldn't have that. And what would he think?

Silas slid his cup forward. "I guess I'd better get back to work," he said, standing. She watched him pull on his coat and zip it all the way up. The old gloves he took from his pockets had holes worn clean through them.

Emily could stand it no longer. "Wait, Silas. I'll be right back."

She hurried into the bedroom and took the gloves from the basket.

"Here, these should help," she said when she

handed them to him.

He turned the thick pair of black work-gloves over in his hands. *"Danki."* His eyes held genuine appreciation as they met hers. He neither smiled nor said another word before turning to the door.

Emily took the soap she'd made for Silas out of the basket. Perhaps she could still give it to him. Slipping the neatly wrapped bar into her coat pocket, she headed over to Silas's house. She knew he would be out at the barn for a while, and it gave her time to clean for him.

She swept the washroom and threw out the old water in the basin. Then she cleaned and filled it with fresh water from the pump in the kitchen. She laid the new bar of soap out for him to find.

It was a joy to clean Silas's house. It was small and the man never dirtied many dishes, taking all his meals at Emily's table, but she never let him know she was doing it. Oh, of course he knew little elves didn't magically pop in when he was in the barn and clean his house for him, but it almost felt like he should, the discreet way she did it. Likewise, Emily hardly ever saw Silas come through her house anymore, yet her wood rack always stayed full.

She threw his dirty clothes into the basket by his bedroom door and made the bed. On wash day she would slip in and grab his basket, too, then she'd hang his things on his own clothesline to dry.

Emily hurried back to her house as she saw Silas coming out of the barn from the window. She quickly took out the ingredients to make Silas's favorite candy. A bit later, he knocked at the door.

"Come in," she said, dusting the powdered sugar off her hands onto the apron.

A brown paper bag was folded down halfway in his hands, containing something flat.

"I brought you something, and I don't really know the protocol on gifts around here…"

She smiled. *He was giving her something?* "It's all right, Silas. I'll forgive your *faux pas*. Gifts aren't needed between friends, but I appreciate the thought."

He held out the package for her to take. Opening it, she found a book with hard covers. She turned it over in her hands. Her fingers ran across the book jacket, full of beautiful flowers embossed into the paper. The cover said, The Helen Steiner Rice Collection. Emily's mouth dropped open. "You found it!" It was her favorite Christian author, a poet with an amazing way of describing God's love.

He smiled. "When you mentioned it, I knew I had to at least look. The bookstore in Asheville special ordered it for me."

"*Viel dank,* Silas, it's just what I wanted."

"You're welcome. You do so much for me. When I think of where I was this time last year…well…I owe you my life, Emily Graber."

"That's sweet of you to say, Silas, but God should get the credit, not me."

"You don't know how big a part you played, then. There's something I never told you."

A haunting look shadowed his eyes and she invited him to sit. She poured him another cup of coffee and sat down by him.

"I almost killed myself last Christmas."

"How?" she asked.

"With my pistol."

She gasped, holding her hand over her mouth. "Silas," she whispered in reprimand.

"I held the gun to my head for an hour. And then, the next thing I knew, I woke up with a plate of food beside me. I don't know how I got there, other than by God's hand, but the plate of food reminded me that there are people who still care about me. And for that, I'm grateful." Silas's eyes spilled out some of the hurt that was inside.

"That's what the tattoo was for," she said. "The one on your arm." It said, *thou shalt not kill.*

"Right. It's a reminder to me every day that God doesn't want me to do that."

She could hold back no longer. Emily took hold of his hands on the table and said, "I don't want you to, either." She swallowed hard. "You're my best friend." Maybe it wasn't appropriate for her to say, but it was true, and she knew he'd understand.

He let out a tired breath. "You're my best friend, too."

She let his hand go, stood by his chair, and gave him a side-hug. Then she put her head down and walked to the counter where she had been working. She turned around and leaned her back against the counter, watching him. They smiled easily at each other a moment before he said he needed to get back to work. Heat rose to her cheeks at the thought of her actions. She shouldn't touch him that way, but it was such a tender moment in their friendship. She wondered if he'd found the soap by the wash basin yet. He was her friend, and she was glad that for once she'd been able to set her carnal desires aside and just be a friend to him. She hadn't realized how much he needed her in his life.

From the bench on the porch, Silas could see Jada's car coming up the drive. He was glad the one-inch of snow that fell the day after Christmas hadn't kept her away.

Jada was dressed in tight pants and high-heeled boots. The kids spilled out of the back, bundled in bright-colored coats, so different from the kids in the community in their dark-colored clothing.

"How are you?" he asked when she walked up to the porch.

"Good. You?" She didn't look good. She wore a fake smile and had lost some weight. *She was too skinny before.*

"The Lord has been good to me. Do you need any money?"

"You don't have any money." Jada shook her head.

Silas's insides burned at her words. She'd cut him down, not even meaning to. "What I have is yours."

"We're fine."

She made no attempt to make small talk, just

gave both the kids a hug and went back to her car.

Silas took the kids inside. "How's Mommy doing?" he asked them.

"Oh, she's just mad at Ryan." Natasha took off her big, pillowy coat and threw it down on the chair.

"What'd he do?" Silas asked.

"It doesn't matter. Ryan says she would yell even if he didn't do anything."

Silas swallowed a laugh. Seems he wasn't the only one Jada couldn't get along with.

"She still not letting you eat any meat?"

Natasha and Will both shook their heads with wide eyes.

"You two up for some turkey and gravy?"

They nodded anxiously.

"Put your coat back on. We'll go over to Miss Emily's. She's waiting for us." As Silas held the kitchen door open for his kids, he prayed he could keep his eyes off Emily. Her whole family would be over, watching him. It'd been easier lately, for some reason, but there were still times when he would get lost in her eyes, and before he even knew what he was doing, he'd be missing his turn in conversation. He couldn't let her find out he had feelings like that for her. It would ruin their friendship, and jeopardize his life in Swan Creek Settlement.

Through the snow Silas tracked, out to the horse stalls. It was difficult keeping up both his horses and Emily's, but he hated to think of the alternative—cooking and cleaning for himself. He worried about his horse that had been sick for days now. He'd sold his others when Jada left, and used the money to keep up the farm. If this one died, he'd be without transportation.

One look confirmed his fears. The old horse hadn't made it through the night. He dragged himself back to Emily's for a cup of coffee and some advice about what to do next.

"You can borrow one of my horses," Emily said simply. "What are neighbors for?"

Silas was beginning to hate hearing the phrase because it always seemed to mean he was down on his luck and his lady-friend was going to have to bail him out. Even Jada looked down on him because of his lack of money.

"What's wrong?" Emily asked, glancing down at the coffee cup in his hand. All this time the woman kept coffee in the house and made it for him, but never drank any herself. *Who does that?*

"This organic farm just isn't making the money I hoped it would. Organic feed prices are through the roof and I'm still having trouble finding people willing to pay extra for the organic label."

Emily touched her bottom lip as she thought, drawing his eyes to them. "Why did you say you quit the organic produce?"

He sighed. "I can't grow anything. I left all that up to Jada."

"Well, I can grow things. I think you could make a lot at the open market this summer with organic produce, and you could contract with the grocery store and even some restaurants. Then you could mention to the buyers that you also have organic meat for sale."

Silas took a sip of coffee, admiring her can-do attitude. "Are you looking to start an organic farm? 'Cause I may have one to sell before the year's out."

She smiled, lightening his mood. "*Nay*, but I could help you grow some produce. We work in the garden together all the time. This would be the same, only bigger."

He shook his head. "Oh, no. I owe you too much already. I've got to make money on my own."

"Well, then make me a partner. I'll take a cut of the pay from the vegetables."

Silas peered into his cup. *Partners, huh?* There wasn't anyone else on earth he could think of he trusted—or wanted to work with. He enjoyed Emily's company, and he *had* been able to control his testosterone around her lately. "You'd have to take fifty percent of the profits or no deal."

She sat up straight in her chair. "You pay me whatever seems fair, but I have conditions, too. No one finds out and it doesn't interfere with my job teaching at the school." She lifted one eyebrow, her bright-blue eyes zeroing in on his.

Her words stopped him. "Is it wrong for us to run a business together?"

She softened her posture, leaning her arms slightly forward on the tabletop. "If there were more people involved, I'd say no. But I doubt either of us wants to answer to the bishop again."

It made sense. And the woman could grow

things. He'd seen it in the garden last season. "Agreed."

"We're going to make plenty of money, Silas."
She smiled a row of beautiful, even teeth.

"I hope you're right…partner." Silas hoped he
was doing the right thing. He prayed God would bless
their efforts, and give him money enough to help Jada
and the kids. But most of all, that he could keep himself
from falling for the girl next door.

Chapter 2

Silas had wasted no time in building a greenhouse out back, and Emily thought he did a splendid job. It was small, with a door in the front, and three tables lining the other sides with shelves above for plants, and below for supplies. With her help, Silas could plant cheaply this year, minimizing their costs, so even if they didn't sell what they'd predicted, there would still be some profit. And if nothing else, Emily would have all the transplants she needed for her garden, feeding them both for the year.

"Feels like spring in here," Emily said as she filled the plastic containers with dirt. It was a warm day for February and the air inside the greenhouse even warmer and more humid, transporting her to days in the garden to come.

Silas had his back to her at the opposite table in the cramped greenhouse. "Your seedlings are up already and mine aren't. What gives?"

She turned around, peering around his arm. "You must have planted them deeper than I did."

He turned around to face her, the closeness both exciting and unsettling, his manly scent about to drive her mad. *I never should have made him that soap.* And she wouldn't have if she'd known it would become a weapon against her.

She gave a tense smile and then turned away, settling her attention back on the dirt cups at hand. They had to quit meeting this way if they were to work together. Behind her, the sound of Silas fumbling with more plastic containers. She hoped he hadn't noticed how uncomfortable she became whenever he neared.

How embarrassing it would be for him to know she loved him, while he only thought of her as a friend.

She reached for the seeds on the far wall as Silas did, their hands meeting at the seed packet, the electrifying current coursing through her. "I'm sorry," she said, not looking at him as she drew her hand back. She knew not to meet his eyes just then, for if she did, she might get hopelessly lost in them, never to be found again.

"You go ahead," he told her, handing the packet out for her to grasp.

"Danki," she said as she took it, his fingers meeting hers once more. Suddenly, their eyes met, and as she feared, she was powerless to resist. She longed for him to hold her again, the way he had once, when she buried her face in his neck. He had only comforted her because Kenny had attacked her, but the memory wouldn't fade. It was wrong and she knew it. She had to be strong, if for nothing else, then for the sake of Silas's business. He needed the money and she needed something to keep her busy this summer, only she didn't realize it would be this hard. She found herself being drawn toward his lips and turned away quickly, letting the task at hand pull her away from her fantasy.

Emily prayed a prayer of forgiveness for letting herself go so far. Perhaps they should take turns working in the greenhouse from now on. She would need to take some sort of precaution because he was becoming more and more difficult to resist.

The beginning of May brought with it cooler temperatures and flooding rains. Silas was glad he hadn't settled any further west, or the rising creek may have prevented him from getting in and out during the wet months.

It was a day of rest, if you could really call any day restful in Amish country. Even on Sundays the chores needed to be done, but only what was absolutely necessary.

He trudged into the house after feeding all the animals and changed his clothes, wet up to the knees from walking through the rain-soaked weeds. There was just enough time to get a warm breakfast at Emily's and head off to church services over at the Wittmer's.

But as he stepped outside once again, he felt something was amiss. Turning his head, he saw two cows in Emily's backyard, one of them standing in the middle of the garden. He ran over, hollering whatever dumb thing came to mind, "Yah," and "get." He got one cow to move from its place, but he nearly slipped as he did, on the muddy edge of the slick garden. His good shoes were now caked with mud.

Emily was soon beside him, barefooted. He wondered how she kept her feet from freezing, but it was May, the month most of the Amish women started going barefoot, regardless of how cold it was outside. She had told him that feet needed to breathe after a long winter.

He watched her chase the cow in the gate that was standing wide open now. His temper flared. Only a single piece of rusty wire had held the gate shut and Silas knew it could break any day, it just happened to be the worst possible day.

"If you'll watch the gate, I'll get a chain," Silas hollered. He hurried to the tool shed and brought back a long chain with a metal clasp to hold the gate shut. He knew there was at least one more cow out, but he couldn't have the rest of them running off when he wasn't watching.

"Stay here and I'll try to bring it around." He left Emily at the gate and slowly snuck past the cow on the other side of Emily's house. He turned and yelled, waving his hands in the air as he came at the cow, sending it jumping toward the gate. Emily opened the gate wide, but at the last second the cow turned and veered right. She closed the gate quickly and ran through the yard after it, Silas making sure it didn't run in the gap between the two houses. Emily had it coming back in the right direction and Silas ran hard to reach the gate before the cow did, dodging a large patch of mud as he went. He let the gate swing wide and ran back to give the cow plenty of room. He and Emily both ran hard after the cow, yelling to drive it in the gate.

Emily slipped, falling down on her bottom in the mud. "Oh," she wailed, looking down at the mess she'd made of herself. The cow was safely in the pasture now and Silas reached a hand down for her.

He felt bad that she had ruined her good church clothes. He knew from what Jada had told him that

Amish women had their nicest clothes set aside for church and other special occasions, even if they did look all alike to Silas.

She took hold, her hand slippery from mud. He reached his other hand down as well, but as it slipped, so did Silas, right in the mud beside her. Heat rose to Silas's face. He'd just changed his clothes and now he would have to change again, not leaving much time for breakfast. *Of all the rotten things to happen…* He turned to Emily. The back of her wrist was hiding her mouth and her shoulders were shaking.

He tried to stand but slipped again. She burst out laughing as hard as he'd ever heard her.

"You think this is funny?" he said, his mood beginning to lighten. She seemed to have that effect on him.

"Ja," she said simply.

Silas picked up a clump of mud and threw it at her, sending her into a high-pitched half-scream. She laughed and threw a clump back at him. All at once, he'd had enough. He took a clump of the wettest mud and got on his knees, bringing it toward her face. She scrambled to get away from him, trying to stand but falling down again.

"Can I give you a mud facial?" he teased.

"Nay," she said in a high-pitched squeal, still trying to get away.

He grabbed her around the waist and pulled her back on the ground beside him. "Hold still. I'll show you how the *Englisher* women do it." He brought the mud closer to her face, causing her to squeal again. At the last second, Silas threw it down and shook out his fingers, Emily lying still beside him.

"You know I wouldn't," he said. He wanted to squeeze her, she was so cute, lying in the mud and squealing like a little pig. For a second, he forgot his lot in life, and he thought he might kiss her. His eyes locked onto hers. Her eyes danced and he caught a glimmer of something. Did she want to kiss him, too? Then she was rolling to the side, away from him, breaking the hold she had on him. He was glad she did, or he might have done the unthinkable. They were only friends and business partners. Never would they be more. Emily was brought up to obey the rules the community had set, and most importantly, God's laws. It was wrong.

He stood carefully and secured the gate. Then they walked back together.

"How are we ever going to get ready for church in time?" he asked.

"There's no way I can," she said, pulling off her *kapp*. "I have mud all the way down to my hair." Her dark-red hair was still pinned up into a tight swirl on her head, making her look both elegant and stately, even with a spot of mud behind her ear.

"Well, look at me," he said, turning his body so they could both see his backside.

She laughed again. "Well, one of us needs to go. What would it look like if both of us were absent?"

She was right. They stopped at the hydrant, to wash Emily's feet and Silas's boots. She followed him inside his house. "It's later than I thought," she said, looking at the clock on the wall. "You'd better hurry."

He could sense a slight apprehension in her voice. He figured she meant it when she said the community wouldn't see it as a coincidence if they both missed church the same day. He took off his shirt and felt the back of his hair.

"There's no time for a bath. Get to the sink," she said.

She began pumping the water out as he lowered his head into the sink. "This is going to be cold."

Cold as ice. He rubbed at his head, trying to clean it quickly in the running water, but before he knew it, Emily had stopped pumping and was rubbing soap into his scalp.

"Is that really necessary?"

"Well, you want to be clean, don't you?" Her tiny fingers clawed at his scalp, pushing his head in a little sway as she worked. He thought he heard a snicker, but couldn't be sure. She rinsed his hair out and then rubbed it hard with a towel, leaving it a little achy but cleaner than it had been in a long time.

"It's fine," he said. She still rubbed the towel at the back of his neck, doting on him like Jada did the kids.

"All right," Emily said, "now get dressed and get out of here as soon as you can. But stop by the house on the way out. I made a cake you can take."

"A cake?"

"*Ja,* I always bake a cake for Sunday services. They'll be expecting it," she said matter-of-factly.

"So what am I supposed to say?"

"Tell them I have a stomach ache. *Nay,* a

headache. And I sent this cake with you. And don't forget to bring back the container." Her index finger touched her bottom lip.

Silas wondered if he should have helped Emily wash her hair so she could've gone instead.

"Snap, snap," she said, bringing him back into action. But he stopped when she walked out the kitchen door, watching her muddy hips sway from side to side.

Clean and dressed once again, he hitched up the buggy and came in for the cake. She handed it to him in a round, plastic container with a small brown paper sack folded down on top.

"What's that?" he asked.

"Your breakfast. You can eat it on the way. Now hurry."

"Should I bring you back a plate?" He really wasn't sure what proper Amish etiquette would be in a situation like this, but he never did, always counting on Emily to tell him.

"Only if one of the ladies sends it with you." She smiled brightly.

"What are you going to do all day?" he asked, reluctant to leave.

She opened her eyes wide. "I'm going to take a bath, now go."

He glanced at her up and down once more before heading outside and climbing into the buggy. She was quite a woman: beautiful, hard-working, determined, positive, and a quick thinker. It was happening, all right. He was falling for her.

Driving away, he felt slight nausea in the pit of his stomach. Hoping it was simply from missing breakfast he opened the bag on the floorboard of the buggy. He pulled out a sausage, egg, and biscuit sandwich and took a big bite. Peeking into the bag, he found two more. She always made sure he was well fed.

He wanted to kick himself for not changing that rusty wire before. Then he wouldn't have the image of Emily laughing at him from the muddy ground lodged in his mind, her slender face beaming at him.

All through church services he thought of her. He told himself it was because the sermon was in Swiss German and he didn't understand a word of it, but deep down he knew better. Emily was starting to get to him and he didn't know what to do about it. It wasn't something he could ask about, either. *So, Bishop, just speaking hypothetically, what should a divorced man do if he accidentally falls in love with his beautiful, single neighbor?* He'd probably tell him to pack up and move away. Not the worst advice, but how could he? It had taken him years to get his farm business going, and no one else would give him rent for free like Emily did. He could buy his own land, but he'd have to go deep in debt, something the Amish taught against.

This was all Jada's fault. If she hadn't of left, the business would be much farther along, and he wouldn't be lonely enough to be tempted by another woman.

Silas let his mind wander during the two-hour sermon. What would he do if Jada came back? His first impulse would be to tell her to take a hike. But knowing he'd be alone the rest of his life wasn't something he was sure he could handle, either. And the community would tell him to forgive her, so he'd probably have to.

Silas thought back to that glimmer he'd saw in Emily's eyes. He'd read her wrong. She was just being nice. All Amish women were insanely nice to everyone, bringing them food and lemonade when they worked, and always smiling. It would be easy to confuse it for attraction. They both knew he was off-limits, so why would she bother? He pushed the thought from his mind and filled the rest of the time with calculations on how much extra money they could make this summer with the produce he was growing.

After dinner, Silas found Emily's cake container and picked it up from the long table.

"Have you heard anything from Jada?" an older woman asked. Silas couldn't remember the woman's name, though she was probably a Schwartz since it was the most common of the last names.

"Just when she drops the kids off and picks them up," he said solemnly. He didn't have the heart to tell her she'd already moved on.

"Well, we'll keep praying," she said as she moved dishes about. Silas never stopped praying for Jada, but his prayers had changed. He didn't pray for her to come back anymore, as apparently some of the community still did. Knowing that wasn't a possibility anymore, he began praying for her to simply turn to God. He didn't know if the bishop would agree or not, but Silas believed now that God wasn't just with the Amish community. He was with anyone who truly believed and accepted Him. And most especially those who tried to do His will.

Silas smiled at the woman. They hadn't made it easy for Jada to come back. Who would want to come back to a community who was shunning them?

Chapter 3

Emily beheld the lush green strawberry bed. "There will be plenty of strawberries next year," she said to Silas.

"Are you sure we don't have to do anything else to them?" he asked from behind her.

"*Nay*, it's God's turn now. We already had plenty of rain, and now the sun is shining brightly again. You cover them with straw in the fall and pull back the straw in the spring. Easy as pie," she said, smiling.

She turned around as he took a step forward, bringing them too close once again. She knew she would need to be especially careful while Silas's children were visiting. They would say anything that popped into their heads to anyone who would listen, without the least bit of censorship. It was nearly the end of their two-week stay for the summer, and Emily was relieved.

Shouts came from the garden beside them. Natasha and Will were chasing each other, giving no mind to the rows of tender young plants. She frowned, causing Silas to raise his voice in a yell. "Get out of the garden!" He shook his head and muttered, "I don't know about those two."

He said that a lot when they visited.

"When we were that age, *Dawdie* would have tanned our hides if we'd of done that."

"I know, but they're at the age now that I'm

afraid they won't want to come if they get mad at me, and I know Jada won't make them."

"Don't you have some kind of legal right to see them?"

"She could fight it and win. I haven't been paying her the money I was supposed to."

"Well, all that's about to change." Emily had faith that they were about to make a lot of money, but she still thought it was a bad idea to not make the children mind. The Bible lessons from their *vater* were the only religious instruction they received now that Jada and Ryan had stopped going to church, and their manners were atrocious. So different than the children that visited her home last summer. But she could understand Silas's reasoning. She couldn't imagine anyone not being allowed to see their own children. It made her despise Jada all the more. Emily knew Jada was a wayward soul and she should be praying for her, but it was difficult when she saw the evidence of the way she treated her family. What kind of woman leaves her husband that way? From what the children had been so freely sharing over the last two weeks, it didn't seem like it would be long before their mother divorced again. Couldn't she stay married to anyone? Simply shameful, it was. Silas had remained pure, and everyone knew it was harder for men, so why couldn't Jada? Had her vows meant nothing?

Emily went inside to cook supper. After tonight, the children would be gone and she could concentrate on setting up a booth at the open market to sell the many vegetables already ripening in the field. She hated to admit it, especially because of how much she adored children, but she would be glad when they had gone.

Silas handed Jada an envelope of money when she came to pick up the kids. It was a step of faith since it was all he had. Emily was excited that their business was doing so well already, since even before she started selling at the open market, they had managed to land a contract with a local supermarket for fresh organic tomatoes, celery, and kale greens. If she was sure this would work out, so was he.

Jada opened the envelope and thumbed through it. He hoped it would please her. Money went much further in the community with no insurance or utility bills to pay, but Jada had quit her job at the lawyer's office soon after marrying Ryan.

"I'll give you some more in a month."

She glanced at him. "I saw the greenhouse out back."

"Yup, you were right about organic vegetables. They're good for you and for the pocketbook."

She gave him a half-smile. "I'm happy for you. You look good."

"The Lord has blessed me."

Her smile faded at his words. "Well, you could lay off the meat a little so you don't have a heart attack before you're fifty."

"Only the Lord knows the number of my days." He liked to watch Jada squirm when he mentioned God, hoping it would make her think of her own eternity and where she would spend it.

"See ya later, Ax." Jada walked to the car, the kids already climbing into the backseat. It was the most pleasant conversation he'd had with his ex-wife since she left.

"It's Silas," he whispered to himself.

Emily was positively giddy when she handed Silas the money she'd made on her first day selling vegetables at the open market. It was only a once-a-week thing, but the money was worth it. "What did I tell you?" she said with a grin.

"That's incredible," he said, looking it. "Jada and I never did this well with produce."

Emily frowned. Did he have to ruin her happy moment with talk of Jada? Now that the children were gone, she hoped to have a peaceful summer. She could handle them fine in small doses, like every other weekend, but the previous two weeks had been a nightmare. After the children went home, she found Silas scrubbing paint off the living room walls where they had decided to make "Daddy's plain house pretty." Emily had thought to offer help, but decided he needed a time-out to think about what he'd done to his children by not disciplining them.

"Well, just wait until the end of the season when you settle up with the grocery store."

Silas was staring at her lips, causing her to touch them in response. She felt a spark from him that she didn't start. Swallowing hard, Emily said, "Take what you need to for expenses."

It took him a moment to answer, "I'll have to check the numbers in the book," but still his eyes flitted from her eyes back to her lips. Could it be Silas was starting to have feelings for her, too? She sincerely hoped not. It was about the only thing that could make her situation any worse.

Trying to avoid Silas while working with him each day was like trying to avoid water in the hottest part of summer; eventually you had to come back to it. Her curiosity was the worst part. Never did she dream it was possible that he would look at her the way she'd been looking at him, but after last Thursday, when she returned from the open market he had. *Hadn't he?* Emily was beginning to doubt what she saw. Did he have feelings for her beyond friendship? And what did it matter other than to make her situation that much more painful?

"I'm going to go fix dinner. Meet me in the house in an hour," she said, wiping the sweat from her forehead. They had been hand-picking tomato worms from the tomato plants for the last two hours, a daily job. He nodded, his dark-eyed glance warming her even more.

Inside the house wasn't that much cooler. Emily washed her face and hands and fanned herself dry with a notebook. Then she started to make dinner. But before she had finished, she heard a car pulling into the drive. Emily's heart stopped. They weren't expecting anyone and Silas was a long way from the house. A quick look outside the window calmed her, but not much. It was Jada's car. What was she doing here? The children had visited last week; it wouldn't be Silas's turn so soon. Unable to keep herself from nosiness, Emily walked outside.

"Have you seen Silas?" Jada asked, the children following close behind.

"He's up in the field." Emily pointed to the other side of the greenhouse where the tomatoes were. She watched Jada and the children start that way, leaving her with no information about why they were there, or how long they'd be staying.

Emily stepped inside to finish dinner, wondering if the children would be joining them today, and hoping it wouldn't be more than a few days.

Jada and Silas didn't come out of the tomato field for a long time. Finally, the children ran down and into Emily's kitchen. Finally, Emily could get some answers, and she wouldn't even have to pry. "Hello, children. What brings you two here today?"

"Mommy's asking Daddy if we can stay here a while," Natasha said.

"Oh, really? Well, more time with your *dawdie*; won't that be nice? Is she going away somewhere?" Emily poured a cold can of soda into two small glasses and handed one to each of them.

"No, she doesn't want us to go back home to Ryan anymore. She said we could live with Daddy until we found an apartment in town."

Emily's mouth dropped open. She wanted to come back here? She closed it quickly. "Well, isn't that nice?" Curiosity was getting the best of her. What would Silas say? She made a plate for each of the children and set it down in front of them at the table. "Excuse me a moment."

Emily slipped into the bedroom and peeked out the window. From a distance, she could see them standing there, talking. Oh, what she wouldn't give to be a field mouse right now, so she could hear their conversation.

When the children finished eating, they ran back up to the field where their parents were, still talking with arms folded. Pretty soon, they all came down toward the house and Jada and the kids climbed into the car. Emily sighed in relief. It was always best when families reunited, but having Jada and the kids on the property from now on was an unsettling thought. Not to mention the way poor Silas would feel when she took off again. He ambled into the kitchen as soon as the car was out of sight, his face ashen.

"Well, what happened?" she asked.

He sat down at his usual place at the kitchen table and when he didn't talk right away, Emily sat down beside him. "Are you okay? What did she say to you?"

"She wants to come back to me."

Emily's mouth dropped open. "And you told her *nay*?"

"No, she's moving back."

She shook her head. "Then, why…"

"I sent her to the store to buy fabric. She's going to have to make all new dresses for her and Natasha. I told her if she was going to live here it would be by my rules." His eyes were hollow.

"You don't look thrilled to have her back," Emily said carefully, her heart beating wildly at the news.

"It'll end just like the last time, but what can I do? She doesn't want to go back to Ryan and she hasn't got the money for an apartment. She's my responsibility. I have to take care of her and the children."

Emily sat there a moment, quiet. She didn't want to see him hurt again, but he was right. He was responsible for his family. "What can I do for you, Silas?" She clasped her hands together on top of the table.

He let out a nervous laugh. "I usually ask you what to do."

Another quiet moment passed while she waited for him to answer.

He sighed. "We can't tell Jada about our partnership."

"I understand," Emily said, though it stabbed at her heart the same.

"Jada can do the work as long as she's here, but I'll still give you the fifty percent like we agreed on."

Emily shook her head. "I can't take money for work I haven't done."

He looked her straight in the eye and placed his hand on hers on the tabletop. "You've been doing her chores for a long time. It's Jada's turn."

Her breath caught at his touch. He was right about that. Emily cooked and cleaned and cared for Silas and his children like they were her own family. But what would she do the rest of the summer without him? Emily held back the tears that were welling up on the rims of her eyelids. "As you wish."

It had been a month since Jada had come to live with Silas again. The Swiss Amish community he now belonged to said that any marriage made after the first was void since marriage vows can only be broken by death. But Silas had rules of his own. He gave his bed over to Jada and Natasha, while he slept in one of the twin beds in the kids' room, telling her he refused to sleep in the same room with another man's wife. He would consider having her back when her divorce was finalized—if she stayed that long.

She was still shunned, and according to the rules, he was supposed to make her eat by herself in the corner like a naughty school-girl. Only Jada hardly ate real meals at all, simply snacking on organic produce around the house and in the field. When she was living with him before, Silas could remember her eating bread and other grains, but now she had decided that gluten was bad for her, and instead of instant organic oatmeal for breakfast, she made everyone in the house eat certified gluten-free steel-cut oats, which were tough to chew and flavored strongly. In a month he had lost nearly ten pounds, his trousers barely fitting anymore. Being hungry all the time made him irritable. He didn't like it and he decided to tell her so.

"How about some bacon for breakfast today?" he told, rather than asked, Jada one morning before walking outside to do chores. After breakfast, Will was going to hang out with him and learn how to run a farm instead of destroying everything in the house. And Natasha was going to have some chores of her own from now on. He'd tried letting Jada do things her way and it didn't work. It was time for him to be a man, and if Jada didn't like it, she could go back to her husband.

Slowly, Emily began to notice a change in Jada. After her shunning was over she was much more submissive toward Silas, bringing him a plate at church dinners and making him lemonade when he worked in the field. But her face didn't hold the glow of a happy housewife, content with her station in life. Instead, she looked more like a servant girl, working for her supper. But Silas wasn't wrong in putting his foot down with her. She would respect him more for it, in the long run. A man needed to act like a man to gain respect, and Emily had to admit, she'd gained a lot of respect for him just by watching. He'd let Jada push him around enough.

When it was time for Silas's annual meat canning frolic, Emily was invited by Jada to attend. It was difficult to be in Jada's kitchen, where Emily knew she'd shared a few private moments with Jada's

32

husband. Like when she'd washed the mud from his hair at the sink. Heat rose to Emily's cheeks at the thought, and she fanned herself with her hand. But Emily had done nothing like what Jada had. How shameful for everyone to know she was an adulteress.

She, Jada, and two other women, had already canned twenty jars of roast beef in the hot kitchen. Emily was gathering things to start another batch when Jada said, "Are you sure we need more, Emily?"

"Never can have enough protein to support a growing family." Emily had meant the growing children; she certainly hoped the family wasn't going to get any new members. The thought threatened nausea. Of course it was what married couples did, but the last time Jada left Silas, he ended up staring down the barrel of a gun, alone, the day after Christmas. Emily hoped he wouldn't let her back into his heart that easily.

Jada didn't say anything, only sighed, and an hour later they had another batch sitting on the counter.

"I believe that's plenty for us for a while. We don't eat a lot of meat," she said. Silas walked in. "Nice work, ladies." He gave his wife a side-hug. "Looks like you're about halfway there," he said to Jada. He smiled and then released her, walking on through the house.

Emily had to turn back to the stove to keep anyone from seeing her holding in a laugh from the look on Jada's face. It almost made Emily feel sorry for her. *Almost.*

Chapter 4

"You did a good job today," Silas said to Jada as she passed by him on her way to bed. They'd accomplished so much since she and the kids had been back.

She stopped. "Thank you," she said and lowered her head, submissively.

"I've missed you, all three of you. It's been nice, being a family again, don't you think?"

She nodded. Her hair was down for the night, black and silky. "Well, good night," she said, and with a slight smile, she disappeared behind the bedroom door.

Silas ran his hands through his hair, stretching his back after a long day's work. He felt good inside—complete. Although Silas missed visiting with Emily, he quite enjoyed feeling like the master of his domain, for once. No longer was he the man who's wife left him, but a man with a family and a successful business to tend to. Jada seemed different now, and in Silas's heart, he began to wish she would stay. He decided to forgive her and take her back into his arms as soon as the divorce was finalized.

Lying awake in his tiny bed next to Will, he thought of what it might be like to hold her again. She was stubborn, and still refused to believe in the one true God, instead, saying things like all roads lead to Heaven, or we'll all end up in the same place eventually, anyway, so why bother? But the Bible said if she was happy to dwell with him then he should allow her to. And that, through his example, she might be saved. That was what he wanted more than anything, to see his whole household saved. It was a scary thought that he might one day enter Heaven's gates and his family would be missing. A chill ran down his back at the very thought. He hated to push her, but it was his responsibility as the spiritual leader of the home to lead the Bible studies after supper. Up until now, he had been studying alone, or with the children. He made up his mind right then to start tomorrow evening, and Jada would attend whether she liked it or not.

Thursdays were the only days Emily could freely talk with Silas. Jada took the kids with her to help sell produce at the open market most of the day, and Silas would come in for a cup of coffee after morning chores and chat awhile.

"Do you think I'm doing the right thing?" he asked.

"What do you think?" Emily wanted him to be sure he was ready to take Jada back and let himself be vulnerable all over again. If she had to, she'd remind him of what happened last time.

"You're right. I need to stop second-guessing myself."

"Silas, you know the Bible just about as well as I do now." And the Bible said he should rule his household—no matter what his wife thought about it. Silas had told her he set certain rules for Jada to follow if she wanted to be his wife again. Emily had been praying for Jada's heart to change, but she hadn't seen it happen in her yet. Only yesterday, when they were picking beans together, Jada had mentioned how she believed God took on many forms. To some, he was Buddha, and to others, Jesus Christ. Emily set her straight right quick that the people didn't believe that at all, and talk like that would earn her a visit from the bishop. That had shut her up for the time being, anyway. It was then Emily realized Jada needed someone to instruct her in their ways, not just shun her for her disobedience.

"But I'll never be able to quote it like you can." He took a sip of his coffee, and Emily set down a piece of Silas's favorite chocolate lava cake in front of him.

"Eventually, you will."

"It's almost time to take some livestock to the market." He smiled.

"I'll pray you do well."

"Well, pray we do well today. Your money's in the vegetables at the open market."

"I still don't feel right taking money for Jada's work." That, and Emily missed having Silas as a friend. She'd take that over money any day. It pained her to see him with Jada again, but she knew it would be the best thing for Silas if Jada would only straighten up and act the part. A man needed a wife—not just a woman who cooked and cleaned for him. Emily would never be a real wife to Silas—maybe not to anyone. The thought sent Emily's arms across her middle, holding the pain inside. She watched the man she loved eat a piece of her chocolate cake.

"I saw you helping Jada pick beans. You do enough. And without your money to get started, we wouldn't have any vegetables to sell."

"*Ja,* but you paid me back for that already. I just wanted to help—not own your business."

"I know. But an agreement is an agreement. Maybe Jada can do all the work next year." With that, Silas stood and turned his coffee cup high into the air, finishing the last drop. "*Danki*, Emily. For everything." It was as if he were saying goodbye forever. Perhaps he was. With Jada here all the time, it wouldn't do for him to be visiting with the single woman next door.

Emily watched him leave, hoping that if it were for the last time, he would find all the happiness in the world, and in return for her unselfishness, it wouldn't destroy her.

Silas liked having a billfold full of money—even if it wasn't all his. He'd done well at the livestock market—very well, and added with the money from the open market stand and the money the grocery store owed him, he almost felt rich. God certainly had blessed him this year. Not only was his business doing well, but his wife and kids were back. He hoped Jada would get her divorce finalized soon so they could remarry, making it official. At least he prayed it would be that easy. In truth, he knew he had a long way to go in rebuilding his relationship with her, but God could handle it. He'd brought her back for a reason, and Silas had faith it was to give him a family.

"How did you do?" Jada asked as Silas came in the kitchen door. He wanted to tease her with a fib, but his smile had already betrayed him.

"You made a lot?"

He nodded.

"A lot, a lot?"

He nodded again. She threw her arms around him and hugged him, her warmth filling a well that had gone dry inside, awakening feelings he forgot he had for her. He pulled her back and caught her eyes, a soft brown. For a second, he expected them to be blue like the sky. His eyes scanned her face for clues, but then she turned away from him.

"The divorce will be finalized soon," she said, facing the sink. It had been months since she'd come to stay and Silas's rules still stood. He'd been sleeping alone in a bed two sizes too small. Maybe soon that could change. Never had he expected to have feelings for Jada again—not after she'd hurt him the last time. He'd only meant to help her out of a sense of responsibility, but now he could see there could be more—if she wanted.

"Marry me." Silas knew she'd been thinking about it. Even now, she was. Jada turned to face him, leaning against the countertop.

"You belong here with me. I can provide for all of us with this farm, with your help."

"You seemed to be doing pretty well before I came along."

She had no idea how much work Emily put into

it.

Jada frowned. "But I have to admit, I've thought about it."

Silas let go of an anxious breath. He had almost convinced her.

"But only if you sell the place."

The wind was knocked out of him like a horse kicking him in the chest. "Why?"

"I don't like what this place has done to you, Ax. Before I married Ryan you said you'd leave the community if we could be together. I'll marry you—if we can leave."

He stared across the small kitchen at the beautiful woman by the sink—his wife. The only wife he'd ever get. This was it. One of those life-changing moments where he'd come to a fork in the road and needed to choose the right path. His first instinct was to go ask Emily. But then he thought of all he'd learned by talking with her and studying the Bible. She would tell him to pray, and so he did. *God, what do I do? My life is yours to do as you please, but tell me now.*

In his heart he knew that if he left the community he wouldn't want to leave its values. She probably still wouldn't like the person he'd become. How long would it be before she'd leave him again? He was a stronger person now, but could he handle the life he had come from? Did he want to? And why was she calling all the shots? Silas remembered the feeling he had of being master of his domain—gone now. She'd taken all the power away from him when she gave him an ultimatum. Now he stood before her, deflated. No, he wouldn't grovel. He wouldn't play games, and he wouldn't leave.

"If you want to be my wife, it'll be here in Swan Creek Settlement. This is a good home—a Christian home, where I can provide for you and our kids. You can go if you want, but if you leave, don't come back." Silas thought he had been firm, but not the least bit angry in his words. He left her in the kitchen to think it over, hoping she would at least consider it.

Emily rushed to the kitchen door where Silas stood knocking at the frame of the screen. It was a warm October day, and the leaves on the trees were colorful and bright. She had finally settled in for another long school year, happy that her thoughts weren't continually on Silas anymore, but after seeing the hurt in his eyes as she let him in, all the feelings she had for him came rushing back. "What's the matter?"

"Jada's divorce is finalized. She got a settlement from Ryan and she's gone to look for apartments." He sat down at the table, and Emily took a seat beside him.

"Oh, Silas, I'm so sorry." And Emily was. As much as she disliked Jada, she was starting to convince herself it was what was best for him, and she was beginning to think it was possible for herself to move on as well.

Silas rubbed his hands over his face. "The Lord giveth, and the Lord taketh away, I guess."

Her heart went out to him. "I really thought she

was going to stay this time," Emily said softly.

"She said we could be together if I left the community."

Emily gasped. "Why would she do that to you?"

"She doesn't like it here—never has. It wouldn't have changed anything between us, though. The problem she has with me isn't being Amish, it's being Christian. And that's not gonna change."

Emily pressed her lips together. Silas hadn't come to her kitchen for coffee and idle chat. He needed reassurance—not from her—from the Lord. "We will all stand before the judgment seat one day to give an account of what we've done. What do you think the Lord will say about your part in this?"

"I think He'll say well done."

"Then worry no more, Silas." She gave him a weak smile.

"I told her if she left, not to come back." He lowered his head. "Do you think God will think that's wrong?" He lifted his head, meeting her eyes.

"I don't presume to know the mind of God. But she did leave you, Silas, and married another. You were patient in having her back the first time."

His eyes flitted around the room. "I shouldn't be here bothering you with my troubles."

"*Nay*, you need a friend right now. Can I make you some coffee?"

"Please," he said, his face wrinkling with red eyes. He put his head in his hands again. Neither one spoke while she made the coffee on the stove, but when she handed him the cup he had regained composure.

"*Danki,*" he said.

Her heart broke for him. Somehow, Jada had managed to do it again. Emily hoped it didn't send him as far down as last time. The thought sank to the bottom of her stomach like lead.

Jada held out her hand to receive the money. Silas counted it twice. He'd paid Emily her share and bought a new horse and some supplies. Now he had everything he needed—except his family. When he turned loose of the money, they'd be gone again. He set the money in Jada's hand. "Are you sure this is what you want, Jada?"

"I can't stay here, Ax. This is no kind of life for me. But you can live in my apartment with us."

"No." The woman was impossible. She wanted everything her way. Getting Silas away from the community was just another way of doing that. "I believe God wants me here."

She frowned.

"Maybe you should pray about this decision before you leave." He'd meant it when he said she couldn't come back. He didn't need a woman toying with his emotions his whole life. He'd be better off alone.

She counted the money. "Aren't I entitled to half?"

Silas gritted his teeth. He'd given her more than half, only she had already figured the numbers herself, and had counted Emily's cut. "I had to bring in a silent partner to help with expenses and such." He didn't know why he felt so low. He'd given her plenty of money to get started with and he knew she had the divorce settlement money to work with, too.

She stuffed the money in her bag with a huff.

"If you'd stay here you wouldn't have to worry about money. I'd provide for you."

"And pump water, and use an outhouse, and can everything over a hot stove? No thanks, Ax. There are much better ways to live, or have you forgotten?"

The blood rushed through his veins. "Goodbye, Jada."

She hollered at the kids and they came in with their bags packed. It felt strange that they didn't even try to hug him goodbye. Perhaps they knew they'd be back soon. Silas hoped that was all it was. Now things would go back to the way they were before, every other weekend and two weeks in the summer while another man raised his kids in the meantime. He knew Jada wouldn't be long without a man, but it would never be him again.

Chapter 5

Emily tiptoed into the house when Silas headed to the barn. She didn't want him to find her there, so she had to hurry. Her pulse quickened. She'd never stolen anything in her entire life, and she prayed God would forgive her for doing it now. Jada left for good that morning and Emily wasn't taking any chances on Silas doing something stupid. She found the pistol on a high shelf, out of the children's reach. She had to stand on a chair to even see it. Bringing the gun down carefully, she laid it on the bed and returned the chair she had stood on to the kitchen. Then she took the gun and held it downward, with her fingers far from the trigger. Her hands began to tremble. What did she know about guns? She figured he kept it loaded. What if she dropped it and shot herself? She swallowed hard. She had to make sure that didn't happen. Silas was in a sorry emotional state, as any man would be if their wife left them. Only Silas had a habit of looking for this gun when that happened, and Emily was going to make sure he didn't find it.

Silas made his way back to the house. He'd forgotten his work gloves and wouldn't think of doing his chores anymore without them. Emily had given them to him last Christmas. The thought of Emily made him realize that the only time he visited with his friend anymore was to complain about his troubles. It hadn't been fair to her. She had helped him through so much and deserved better. Maybe he could bring her supper the next time he had to run to town, so she wouldn't have to cook. He hated it, but he figured she'd start cooking for him again. He loved her cooking, but he hated being such a burden to her.

He walked through the house, but a dull thud in the other room stopped him. An eerie sensation that someone was in the house seeped through. He took a step toward the bedroom and swallowed hard. Finally, he took a chance, "Emily?" He waited for her to say something.

Silence.

Hands balling into fists, the blood rushed through his veins. He pushed open the bedroom door with a soft creak. A gun was pointed at his legs. Silas took a sidestep to the right, just inside the doorframe. Emily stood holding his revolver with shaking hands and a ghastly look. He grabbed the gun from her. Releasing the cylinder with a quick click, he shook out all five rounds onto the bed, then set the gun back up on the shelf. Then, he took Emily by the upper arms as she began to sob. "What did you think you were doing?" His voice rang out in the small room.

She flinched at his words. "I was trying to steal it," she said behind tears, not meeting his eyes.

Silas could tell by the careless way she held the revolver she didn't know the first thing about guns. What kind of game was she playing? She could have killed either one of them if she'd dropped it, causing it to go off. And what was she doing going through his things like that? He shook her arms. "Why?"

She covered her face with her hands, but Silas removed them, holding onto her wrists. "Why?" he said even louder, leaning down and forcing her eyes to meet his.

"I was afraid you'd commit the unforgivable sin," her tiny voice said.

The unforgivable sin. She was afraid he would kill himself. He let out a tense breath.

Her clear blue eyes watered, reminding him of the one time in his life he saw the ocean. It was during his wilder days before he married Jada. He'd hitchhiked all the way to Florida on a journey to find God, before he knew God was everywhere. He got involved with the wrong people, made even more bad decisions, and found himself on the beach without a dime to his name. He wanted to die. Then he saw the clear blue water, and for some reason that to this day he still didn't know, he'd changed his mind.

He let go of Emily's wrists and pulled her to himself tightly, as if hanging on for dear life. His eyes darted around to the open door, but it was unlikely anyone would visit now. Silas had never had a better friend. "I'm sorry, Emily," he said with his hand on her *kapp*. "I didn't mean to scare you," his voice broken. He shifted his weight back and forth, holding her as she wept on his shoulder with her arms around him tight.

Emily tried to smooth the awkwardness in the room at supper. She had apologized for taking Silas's gun and promised not to touch it again, but the way he'd held her had rekindled the fire that threatened to consume her. The months spent far away from Silas felt non-existent now as he sat in his usual place at the table. He eyed her as she brought food from the stove to the table. After prayer, Silas said, "About earlier…"

"I promise never to do it again." Her eyes refused to look up. "Will you please forgive me?"

"I was going to ask if you wanted to learn to shoot."

"Me?"

He nodded. "If you're going to handle one, you need to know how to be safe with it."

"I don't know, Silas." Her face was hot with embarrassment from the day already. She hadn't planned on embarrassing herself further.

"You may need to know how sometime. Never know what can happen out here."

She shook her head. "*Dawdie* never allowed any of us girls to handle a gun. He said it wasn't proper."

"You're a grown woman now, and your *dawdie's* not here." His words were kind, with no disrespect to *Vater*, and they were true, but still, she was hesitant.

"I don't believe in killing."

"What about a snake?" he said.

"I'd hope my neighbor would help me."

He laughed, breaking much of the tension in the room. "Then just for fun."

After supper and Bible study like old times,

Silas took Emily to the far side of the property and stood facing an open field with a hillside in the back of it. He explained to her how a bullet would keep traveling for miles until it hit something, and showed her how to load and unload it. Then he handed it to her.

"I don't think I can." Emily's hands began to shake.

"Here." Silas wrapped his arms around her and held the gun with her hands stretched out in front. "Keep the back of your hand down, so it doesn't get pinched. Now, I want you to aim for that tree over there. Got it?"

"I think so."

"Good." He placed his finger over hers on the trigger. "I'm going to help you. Ready?"

She gave a tense nod before Silas pulled the trigger, causing a blast that rang in her ears. She'd done it. Adrenaline coursed through her, leaving her both confident she could conquer anything she set out to do and terrified all at the same time. "I did it!"

She turned around, passing the gun to Silas as she did. "I really did it!"

"Of course you did," he said, standing very close. "And you'll do it again and again until you're comfortable using it."

Emily gazed into his eyes. "You're different this time."

"What do you mean?"

"I mean I shouldn't have worried about you this time. Am I right?"

He took a step back, breaking the hold that was forming between them. "No. I've got something this time I didn't have before. God—and you."

Straw was strung over the long strawberry bed. Silas whistled a tune as he threw the clumps down and watched Emily pull them apart with slender white fingers. Ever since Silas had caught Emily in his bedroom holding a loaded gun, he'd been different. Something about the selfless act of love had brought a change in him he hadn't expected. He figured on moping around the house after Jada and the kids left, but this time he had a spring in his step, and he was determined not to let it go. Jada would do what Jada would do, and he'd always feel responsible for her, but he wouldn't live with her anymore. He was content to remain alone the rest of his days—as long as he had God on his side, and good friends and neighbors like Emily Graber.

Emily began to yodel to the tune, high-pitched and happy. Silas thought back to how his feelings had changed for her over the years. When he met her, she was a little girl of fifteen. When her father died, she had quickly become his advisor and best friend. Now she was more than that, but what? Silas wasn't sure. He cared for her deeply, more than any friend he'd ever had, and in some ways, even what he'd experienced with Jada. She was family…and sometimes he had to fight the urge to kiss her. Maybe this was the kind of relationship people described as complicated. He knew he loved her, but loving her like a man loves a woman wasn't permitted. He thought back to the way he'd held her close. By Emily's actions, Silas was beginning to wonder if that was exactly how Emily would describe their relationship, too. He may never know for sure.

"In about six months we'll have the biggest mess of strawberries you've ever seen." Emily stood, wiping the dust from her face with her dress sleeve.

"Sounds good to me," Silas said. "There's a little time before supper. Want to get some target practice in? I can set up a tin can and we'll see how good you can aim."

Her eyes were tenderly on his. "I'd like that," she said softly, as it if were a pleasant surprise. Learning to use a gun was a life-skill everyone in the country needed to know, male or female. You never knew when you'd need to defend yourself from someone or some thing. And Silas had to admit, he enjoyed spending time with Emily.

With cotton stuffed in Emily's ears, she held the gun straight in front of her. If she could keep from jerking when she pulled the trigger she could hit the can. Every day for almost a week she'd been trying, but Silas had told her the short-barreled guns were harder to hit with. She pulled the trigger slowly, causing a loud bang that rang in her ears but didn't scare her much anymore. The can remained standing, mocking her.

"I think it's the half-moon sights. Let me show

you." Silas tossed his hat to the ground and took a step forward, holding his arms around her back, and grabbing her hands that held the gun. His warmth was suddenly more than Emily could take and she began melting to his body, her breathing labored and her arms lowering. He pulled them back up to aim. "This right here," he pointed to the sights, "should be in line with this one." He pointed to the other sight, but Emily struggled to pay attention. She turned her head to the right, his cheek directly beside her, giving off a musky smell that made her almost dizzy. The ends of his beard tickled her face. He turned his head, suddenly so close Emily couldn't stand it. She moved away, handing him the gun, and said, "I need to get back home." Then she ran through the field as fast as her legs could carry her.

Silas watched Emily run through the field, knowing full well what had happened. He picked up his hat and gave Emily a good head start before heading back, himself. He'd almost kissed her, only this time he could tell she wanted to kiss him, too. And from the looks of it, she'd gotten away just in time.

How long? Silas thought back to the times they'd shared together, trying to figure out when Emily had fallen for him. The summer before last she was dating that twit, Nelson. And Jada had been here for months. That still left a lot of time between.

He walked through the field slowly, carrying the gun in one hand. All this time, Silas had been so concerned with his own needs and wants, never once giving thought to Emily's. His heart-rate sped as he thought of it. A beautiful woman, all alone in the world, pining for him. Normally, he would be proud, his ego blown up like a hot air balloon, but after living with the Amish all these years, he saw it as a problem. A big problem—but only because he felt the same about her.

Desperately trying to think of an excuse for her behavior, Emily pulled out the pots and pans to make supper. Could she say she hadn't felt well? Or maybe that she had something in her eye? Those were horrible excuses and she knew it, but Silas would be coming in soon and she'd need to say something when he asked. She couldn't tell him what was really on her heart. She'd lie through her teeth first, and who could blame her?

She finished fixing supper and then paced the room, thinking. She'd say nothing if *he* didn't, and if he did, she'd say she thought she forgot something on the stove. It was a careless mistake, one she would never make herself, but she knew others who had, and she was willing to play the part of a silly, forgetful girl to get out of this one.

Silas watched Emily squirm in her chair under his gaze. He hadn't meant to make her uncomfortable, but he couldn't help staring. He still didn't know what to say to her. Maybe nothing at all? "This is good chicken," Silas said. "But everything you make is good."

"Danki," she said, not looking up.

Her meekness was as attractive as her dainty figure. He waited a few minutes for her to speak. When she didn't, he said, "You know, you don't have to cook for me all the time."

Her eyes were still on her plate. "I enjoy cooking for you."

"Well, I think you're quite a woman. I just wanted you to know that." What was he saying? Was he trying to make things worse?

"I have the highest respect for you as well, Silas. You're a good neighbor and friend." She picked at her mashed potatoes and gravy with her fork. She knew her place. It wasn't appropriate for her to say more. Still, Silas wondered what she would say if she were allowed.

"You're not eating much," he said.

Emily's eyes came to life and she took a big bite. It was obvious she was hiding it. Silas finished his meal quietly. He didn't know what to do, and for the first time, he couldn't ask Emily for advice.

Emily busied herself with school projects that kept her after hours, planning, grading, organizing. She hardly had time for much else. During Christmas break, she'd stayed with her sister for a week, and although Silas had come for Christmas dinner, she was able to contain herself, keeping her desires wrapped up tightly and well-hidden. She couldn't let Silas know how she felt. Doing so would only give him an unfair advantage over her. And how awkward would he feel, knowing she loved him and not feeling the same way about her?

It was late January, and some of the *Englishers* from town had sent word that an ice storm was approaching. Since the air was bitterly cold, Silas had offered to go into town, bringing back supplies to last them for a couple weeks, just in case.

Henry had visited and wanted Emily to come ride out the storm with his family, but Emily had turned him down, saying the Lord would provide for her needs.

Now she stood looking out the kitchen window, waiting for Silas to finish morning chores so she wouldn't have to worry about him. At first the ice fell as little balls, bouncing off the roof onto the cold ground, but then it had changed to rain, and Emily knew that if it happened like they expected it to, tree limbs would crash to the ground. No one would go anywhere in the buggy for many days, and even walking outside would be hazardous. Without a phone, a person couldn't even call for help if there were an accident, making Silas and Emily that much more important to each other.

Silas burst through the door, shutting it hard behind him.

"What took you so long?" she asked.

"I did the morning chores and the evening chores, too. The animals all have enough to last them, but I'll have to break their water again tomorrow sometime." He took off his coat and hung it on the back of the kitchen chair.

Now that Silas was safe, they just needed to wait until the storm passed. She poured Silas a hot cup of coffee. "We may as well make ourselves comfortable," Emily said, handing it to him. "Would you like to sit in the living room today?" Of all the times Silas had been in and out of her house, she'd never asked him to sit in the living room, opting instead for the kitchen table, where he could easily bolt out the kitchen door if he needed to, to escape the appearance of evil. But today was different. Not a soul would be stirring in the settlement today, and they could relax without wondering who might drop by. Emily had on her house *kapp*, thinner and not nearly as stiff, allowing a small bit of her hairline to show in the front. She'd left her shoes by the door, instead opting for warm socks to keep her feet warm on the hard floors of the house.

Emily could tell Silas was more comfortable in her living room. Not long after they sat down and started conversing, he began telling her things about himself he'd never shared before. His name was Ax Chase Moreland and his parents were hippies. His *vater* disappeared when he was young and his *mueter* couldn't keep the same man for more than a year at a time. One of his *mueter's* boyfriends had burned him with the end of a cigarette when he was nine, leaving a scar on his back. He later decided to cover it with an ax and a snake.

"You don't even remember what your *vater*

looks like?" Emily asked.

"No. But it doesn't matter anymore. Grown men don't need a father." His face would say different.

Everyone needed someone. "What do you think you'd be doing if you weren't here."

He grew quiet a moment.

She didn't mean to pry. "I'm sorry, Silas. We can talk about something else."

"What about you? What's your story?"

She laughed, lifting her palms upward and out to her sides. "This is it. Terribly interesting, isn't it?"

But Silas's face was still serious. "Why haven't you married yet?" his voice soft.

She cleared her throat and then didn't miss a beat to give the line she'd practiced. "I don't want to leave my school children."

Silas took a sip of coffee. "But there must be times when you doubt your decision, right? I know I would."

"*Ja,* sometimes." Her eyes fell on him as she took a deep breath. "We've sat here until we almost missed dinnertime." Emily stood. "I'll have your dinner ready in two shakes of a lamb's tail," she said, trying to sound upbeat.

In the kitchen, Emily pulled out pots and pans, but before she even turned around, she knew he was behind her.

"Can I help?" He spoke in a husky whisper.

"With dinner?" she asked, already unnerved by his presence in her kitchen.

"You've cooked a lot of meals for me. Least I could do is help."

"Cooking is women's work. You really don't need to trouble yourself with it." Emily went to the cabinet and pulled out some spices, but when she turned back around, Silas was in front of her, his dark, haunting eyes pleading, threatening to rip her heart out if she stared at them a moment longer. The intensity of it jolted her, causing her to draw in a deep breath and tense her whole body. She caught the scent of bergamot and cedarwood, heightening her awareness of him.

Silas grabbed her wrists, and the plastic spice bottles fell with a double thud on the hardwood. He ran his hands down hers until their palms met, sending a delicious tingle all down her. With intertwining fingers he directed them, pushing her hands upward and into the cabinet, on both sides of her head. Her breathing had stopped the second he touched her, and now she craved air, drawing in an audible breath. Was this really happening?

Leaning down, his lips met hers with a maddening force, holding her captive in their grip. She fought back, but not to get away. What she once thought was a fire inside, she now knew had only been a spark. But the blaze Silas set now threatened to consume her.

He stopped only to mutter, "Say it," then kissed her again; she released herself once more to his commanding lips. When he drew back the second time, she gasped in a sharp breath, "Say what?" He kissed her throat, then under her ear, and let go of her hands. She wrapped them around his massive arms that could make any task look like child's play, feeling the tenseness of his hard muscles.

"The verse," he said between slow kisses. He pressed closer. "You must have twenty." Hot breath on her neck melted her. Had it not been for the tall cabinet at her back she may have fallen to the floor.

Emily's mind drew a blank. Of course she knew what they were doing was wrong. *So wrong.* He fingered her cheek with a warm hand, and then her hair beneath the edge of her *kapp*. Surrendering to all the times she'd dreamed of this, she buried her face in his neck and breathed a kiss there, before he found her lips again.

Her conscience nagged at her total disregard for what was right. "Silas," she said breathily, trying to pull herself away. She kissed him again, letting his mouth linger on hers, "We can't," she whispered on his lips.

She met his eyes and he breathed the words, "I know," before kissing her again, his lips warm and so inviting. "But tell me why. I need to hear it."

She ran her fingers through the dark mass of his brown hair as she pulled him in once more, already missing the feel of his mouth on hers. Emily knew she had to stop, but never had she dreamed a kiss could make her feel so alive. Her knees weakened as she pulled away, and she was left shaking from the inside out. Lightly panting, his body still pressed to hers, she whispered, "It will destroy our souls."

Her words stopped Silas cold, and hung on the small span of air between them. Dropping her arms down to hold him tightly around the waist, she could feel one of his hands on her back and the other on her *kapp*.

"Will you show me? Where it says that?" His voice a broken whisper. He was still holding her, his chest moving up and down, the sound of his heart a drum from a distant land. She nodded in his hand, savoring the moment, reluctant to let go of the warmth of his body, knowing it would be for the last time. They couldn't do this again. Not only had she let it go too far, but apparently Silas had, too.

Silas had done the right thing, not stepping foot in Emily's house while she was there. Not once since the big ice storm had they been alone in a room together. Instead, she brought his meals to his porch or set them on the table of his house before he came in. He'd done a horrible thing by kissing Emily, and Silas wished there was someone to confess to so he could unburden his soul. He'd asked God for forgiveness, but what good did it do when he couldn't stop his mind from reliving the sensation? She smelled like honeysuckle on the vine and her lips were soft as wool.

Silas didn't even know what had come over him that day, but he'd successfully managed to complicate matters much more than they already were. And now there was no turning back. He'd left her kitchen in a hurry when they were finally able to tear themselves apart from their lengthy embrace. He'd apologized and headed outside, not knowing what else to say. The whole first week, not a word was said. Now each time their eyes met, they shared a mutual knowing of their sin.

The ice was beginning to melt, leaving a muddy mess in the yard. Silas knew Emily would be bringing him a plate any moment, risking a slip in the mud to make sure he was fed. He remembered the first time she ventured out after their lips had acquainted with each other. She had socks on over her shoes to walk to his porch, leaving a plastic-wrapped plate of chicken and gravy with a small paper taped to the top. On it were Bible references, the ones he'd asked for. Silas hadn't grown up Amish, but he took this way of life seriously. How much more so did Emily?

Wrapping the plate with shaking hands, Emily turned to the door, where *Dawdie's* old mud-boots awaited. She stopped short when she saw Silas coming her way. Had he decided to come in for supper? Should she allow it? Already, her soul bore the mark of an adulteress. She was no better than Jada in God's eyes.

A rap at the screen sent a jolt through her heart. He caught her eyes through the window and opened the first door, lightly knocking on the second. Finally she opened it, but not all the way.

"You don't have to make me any food, not ever if you don't want to. I don't want you to think…"

She watched him swallow hard as the cold air whipped at her ankles. She turned and grabbed the plate on the table and handed it to him, barely meeting his eyes as she did.

He exhaled loudly. "Are you all right?"

She'd barely uttered one word to him since it happened, reliving the scene in her mind daily and wondering how she'd forgotten her raising so quickly. Silas's eyes were tender, but they provided no comfort. Her sins were her own.

She shook her head in answer to his question. She wasn't all right, and may never be again.

"Is there anything I can do for you, Emily?"

"Just stay away." She pressed her lips together in a slight smile, but tears were coming on quickly. She lifted one hand over mouth as she closed the door.

Chapter 6

Spring came without another word from Silas. A routine formed. Silas never allowed Emily to carry his plate to him in bad weather. Any rainy, or snowy day he would come to her house and she would hand it to him through the open door. During the day when she was in school, he would bring in her wood, and leave the eggs on the counter. Then he would make himself scarce while she cleaned and swept his house before making supper. It had become a way of life to care for each other this way, but Emily missed talking with Silas over supper, and most importantly their Bible studies together.

So on a bright day at the end of April, Emily decided it was time to reclaim her friend once more. She brought his covered plate to his door and knocked. Silas answered quickly, no doubt wondering what could be wrong for her to do so.

"It's nice outside. Would you like to take your supper on the front porch today?" she asked, her eyes bouncing on the ground a bit before looking up and meeting his.

He nodded and stepped outside, taking the plate from her hands. She turned on her heels and strode to her kitchen door, filling her own plate before heading through the house to the front porch. Silas was already seated on the top step as Emily breezed through to sit on the swing.

They prayed over their food and Emily began

eating, watching Silas from the corner of her eye. Months had passed, yet it seemed like only yesterday he'd held her close. She pushed the thought aside. If she was going to make this work, she would have to let herself forget.

"How's it going in the greenhouse?" she asked.

"Not the best, but I'm managing," he mumbled.

"Maybe you should hire some help," Emily said, trying to sound like she didn't care either way. She wanted to help him but knew they wouldn't be able to manage it.

"How are you?" he asked.

She glanced up from her plate, but only for a second. "Better." She'd finally managed to make peace with God and herself about the situation, telling herself it was simply because she hadn't done any experimenting while in *Rumspringa*. Never would she have dreamed it. Having been raised in a strict household, they were taught not to kiss or even touch a *beau* until engaged. No one had ever proposed marriage to Emily, and her first kiss was a red-hot mess during an ice storm. As exciting as it was, it left her emotionally drained and spiritually unsettled. Yet the heat of it still rose up in her now and then.

"How are you?" she ventured to say.

"I'm still waiting for you to forgive me."

She met his eyes boldly. *He's taking the blame?* "It was my fault."

"No. I kissed you, remember?"

She gazed down at her hands, remembering the way he forced them to the cabinet, so in control of the situation. She stopped herself before the memory replayed further. "I forgive you."

"I'll never forgive myself," he said.

"God is faithful to forgive those who ask. You should strive to forgive, too, even yourself." She'd had to come to the same conclusion recently.

"I miss you."

"I miss you, too, Silas." Every moment of the day she missed him.

He sighed. "Maybe I should sell the place."

A silent tear fell into her plate before she even knew it was on its way. "*Nay,* I'll sell." She sniffled.

"You can't sell, this is your family's land."

"Then I'll give it to one of them. I could never live here alone."

"And I couldn't stand it knowing you were alone."

"Then what do we do?" she asked. She took a deep breath to calm herself, setting the plate from her lap to the other side of the swing and hanging her head low.

"We just need to keep our distance."

Her chest flooded with relief. He wasn't leaving and he still wanted to be her friend. As hard as it was to love Silas knowing he would never be hers, it would be infinitely worse to lose him altogether. "As you wish."

Silas watched Emily nearly go to tears when he told her about the dead tree in the side yard. Lightning had struck it, causing the already top-heavy tree to split down the middle beneath the weight of its too-heavy branches. She'd only began speaking to him again a few days ago and he hated to push it, but he needed to know how to proceed.

She sat on the edge of the strawberry bed, where she was uncovering the straw from the plants. "It was my favorite. As children, we climbed and played on it, and used its seed pods as pretend food." Then she got a faraway look in her eyes.

"What kind of tree is it?" Silas asked.

"A mimosa."

"Are they good for anything?" He tilted his head to the side.

Her eyes narrowed at him. "It was sentimental."

He was only trying to be practical. Maybe another approach. "What would your father tell me to do with it?"

She turned back to the strawberry bed, shaking her head in defeat. "Burn it."

He went back to the side yard and spent the afternoon chopping away at the dead tree. He loaded the wheelbarrow full and made trip after trip across the yard to the woodchopping stump. When he came to the largest part of the trunk, he decided to make something of it. He was no woodworker though, so it would have to be something simple. Silas wheeled the large chunk of wood to the corner of the barn when Emily wasn't looking. He would hate for her to get her hopes up that he could do something with it and then find out he couldn't. Silas wiped the sweat from his brow and replaced his hat. That project would have to wait for another day. He'd seen some of those trees growing along the roadside before, and he knew just where to find them.

Emily tried to take her mind away from the loss of her beloved tree. The cool-weather crops were doing well, and it wouldn't be much longer before school would be out and Emily would be planting tomatoes. She hoped Silas could make his business work without her. If he could, he was sure to make a healthy profit. Working with him now would not only be unwise, but risky. No one could find out the feelings Emily and Silas shared.

After Emily carefully uncovered each strawberry plant, tucking last winter's straw neatly around each one, she weeded around the fragile lettuce leaves, taking some inside with her when she went to start supper.

After she had washed each lettuce leaf for the salad, she saw Silas leaving in the buggy. It wasn't like him to go anywhere and not tell her where, or when he'd return. Emily thought it peculiar, but it reminded her of how loosely their ties were bound. He was a grown man with a life of his own and she wasn't his wife. He owed her no explanations for any of his actions. The thought brought her pause. What was she doing with a man she had no future with? Had she gone mad? What would *Mawmie* and *Dawdie* say if they were here? Then she remembered what *guete* friends *Dawdie* and Silas were. Perhaps he'd tell her to be a friend to him. She hoped.

When supper was ready she waited, impatiently tapping her fingers on the kitchen table. Where was he? They had been taking their suppers on the front porch the last few days, eating out in the open air, away from the privacy of the enclosed walls of the house.

Emily glanced at the spice cabinet, a place where her mind would forever remember her forbidden ecstasy. She drew in a deep breath and stood. Then she spotted Silas's buggy coming up the drive, stopping in front of the house. He jumped out and Emily rushed to meet him in the yard.

"You know anyone who's good with plants?" he asked.

She raised an eyebrow in question.

"I've got a little tree here that needs a good home." He pulled out a three-foot mimosa sapling from the back of the buggy, tied at the bottom with a burlap sack. "I got all the roots I could get. I'll dig the hole, but it'd probably be better if you did the planting."

So that was where he'd been. Her eyes were starting to feel misty when she said, *"Danki."* No one had ever been so thoughtful to Emily before, and right then Emily decided husband or not, she'd never settle for anyone less caring. She wondered how she'd ever be able to leave Silas alone, but somewhere in the back of her mind she figured she'd have to find a way. eventually. Not this year or even the next, but some day she would need to. How could either of them stand to live this way forever?

Silas nodded in the quiet way he had about him, his dark eyes a beautiful, rich brown in the sunshine.

Emily showed Silas where to dig the hole and soon a new tree was planted, not far from where the old one once stood.

"There," she said, patting the soil down around the tree. "It just needs watered."

He smiled tensely. "Now your children will have a mimosa to play on, too."

She stood and met his eyes boldly. The hurt she felt was mirrored back in the face she saw. So the thought didn't live only in the back of Emily's mind.

"How long do they bear?" Silas asked Emily, looking fascinated by the bumper crop of strawberries before them.

"A few years, and then they'll die out if we don't make sure they make new plants."

"How do we do that?"

She smiled coyly. "Make a new strawberry bed."

He shook his head. "Too much work."

She shrugged her shoulders. "You asked." It didn't matter to her one way or the other. She got a bowl and picked strawberries until it was so full they began to tumble down. She'd see what he thought about it after he had dessert.

Bringing the bowl into the kitchen, she grabbed

two more and headed back out. Silas took one from her and they began to pick berries as they talked, each of them coming closer to the corner of the bed where they finally met. His hand brushed hers, and like an electrical current, it shot up her arm.

"I'm sorry," Silas said. "I didn't mean to."

She could see the respect in his eyes. Turning toward him, she felt his pull. Emily wanted to yield to her desires, but could still feel the sting of their sin like it was yesterday, though in reality, it had been months.

"Don't," he said, shaking his head. "Don't look at me that way." His words were rough, but his voice soft.

"Me?" Her eyes flitted around like there was a possibility there could be someone else. "What did I do?"

"That thing you do with your eyes."

"What thing?" She stared at his moving lips as he talked, wanting badly to touch them.

"That flirty look you have."

She put her head down, suddenly feeling like a student in the corner. "I'm not trying to flirt with you. I never was."

Silas went back to picking berries. "I know," he said lowly. "That's what makes you so irresistible. You're attractive without even trying to be." He threw the strawberry in the bowl hard enough to bruise it.

She glanced at the battered berry and then back to Silas. "Are we going to be okay?"

He didn't look up from his work. "No. But you are."

Emily struggled to understand, picking a few

more berries as she thought. Finally, she gave up and asked, "What does that mean?"

"You need to get married."

He still wasn't looking at her, so he couldn't know her mouth had dropped open. "I've decided to remain single to keep my job as school teacher."

Silas smiled and gazed at her with a soft laugh, his eyes glistening. Then he said in hushed tones, "No one who wants to stay single kisses like that."

Silas had bickered with Emily for months about her singleness. He thought about it while sitting on the bench outside his door, waiting for Jada and the kids to arrive for their two-week summer stay, before school started back again. It wasn't right for someone like Emily to remain single. She was so fragile and beautiful—inside and out. It burned him with jealousy to think of her with another man, but he'd burn himself in other ways if he didn't encourage it. Part of him was enjoying the life he had with Emily as it was. She took care of him, cooking for him, cleaning, even cutting his hair. But she deserved better. She needed someone to come in each night before supper and kiss her hard on the mouth just to let her know someone still loved her. Something Silas would never be able to do. The time would soon come for them to separate and he feared it more than anything else that could possibly happen. Where would he find a friend like her? How long before she forgot the special bond between them?

Jada's car pulled into the drive and all three of them hopped out. Jada was wearing a pair of her shortest shorts. He knew they had to be the shortest because they couldn't possibly make them any shorter than that. Her blazing red tank top revealed a belly button ring when she walked. He knew she looked sleazy dressed that way, but he was a man with a pulse. Tearing his eyes away, he stood to greet the kids. "Having a good summer?" he asked.

They both shrugged their shoulders, absorbed in their devices. Natasha had a phone and Will had some sort of game player.

"How are you?" he asked his ex-wife.

"Good."

"Well, you're glowing, you must be eating well." He watched her face turn red as a cherry tomato.

A knowing crept in. "Kids, you can go on inside, I'll be there in a minute." Silas held the door open for them. "It's not just a new diet, is it?" Silas knew Jada was always trying some new diet she found online or in a health book, keeping up-to-date on the latest research for diet and fitness, but he'd hit on something more, and by her reaction, he already guessed what.

"Yes, I'm pregnant, but it's still early and I haven't told the kids yet. How did you know?" Jada crossed her arms in front of her.

"You just…always looked prettier when you were pregnant." It felt out of place for him to say, even though they had been married for years and already knew each other's intimate secrets. In the Amish community, no one spoke of pregnancy—like it didn't exist or something. And when a couple showed up for church the next Sunday with a bundle in their arms, people acted all surprised like they had no idea they were expecting. He watched Jada twirl her black, shoulder-length hair around her finger.

"So, who's the father?"

"A man named Carlos, as if it's any of your business," she said between clenched teeth.

"And he—"

"We're not together."

Silas nodded slowly. "Are you going to be okay? Do you need money?"

She sighed, letting her guard down finally. "There's a lot of help for single mothers without much income."

Silas frowned. He didn't want his family living off state assistance. Not that there was anything wrong with needing help, but he worked hard to provide for them. He pulled out his billfold and gave her some money. "I'll have more after I go to the market in the fall."

She took the money and poked it in her tight little pocket. "Thanks."

He made her come in and filled a sack of vegetables for her from what he had picked that week and left on the kitchen table. "You need to eat better, Jada."

"I eat much healthier than you do," she said in a high-pitched voice.

"I'm sure eating all organic produce is fine for you, but *the children* need more." He opened his eyes wide and stern as she took the bag.

"Thank you," she said. "I'd better get going. Don't you two gorge yourselves on too much meat and soda," she said, pointing to each of her children. They both cringed. Silas made a face when her back was turned, indicating he hadn't told. This caused them to smile, and Jada, in turn, to shoot him a narrow-eyed look.

"What?" he said, idiotically, bringing a smile to Jada's face. The children laughed.

Silas prayed for Jada as she drove away, knowing the road she chose was her own, as difficult as it would be.

"Jada's...with child?" Emily's face was hot from talking about it. Her eyes opened wider than ever. She sat on the porch swing, while the children played tag in the yard.

"The children don't know yet," he said from the top step, glancing at them.

"As well they shouldn't." Emily stared at Silas in astonishment.

He shrugged his shoulders. "What? It's not mine. I haven't known her in the biblical sense for years now."

Emily's eyes threatened to fall right out. He hadn't been with Jada when she stayed with him for months? This was all so dramatic. Even the ladies at work frolics didn't share this much. "And she didn't remarry?"

Silas shook his head.

The naughty girl. "How's she going to find a husband now?" she asked.

"I don't know that she's looking."

Emily's mouth dropped open. She would never understand *Englisher* women. Emily stood and gathered a stack of plates from supper with Silas and the children.

Silas hollered for Will. When he came running up to him Silas said, "I want you to go with Miss Emily to the kitchen and she'll give you some scraps to take out. Do as she tells you with them."

Will held the door open for her, showing some improvement on his manners from summers past when he'd nearly driven her mad.

Inside the kitchen, she scraped all the vegetables into a bowl and the meat bones into a pan. Then she told him what to do with each. "The vegetables go in the compost heap by the garden. The meat scraps go far away from the house, at least over the first fence, so they won't draw in critters. Do you understand?"

He nodded.

"*Guete* boy." She held the kitchen door open for him and watched him hurry across the yard. Then she pulled the lemonade pitcher out of the fridge and brought it to the front porch where Silas sat.

"So, what will she do?" she said, pouring.

"She'll probably live off state assistance until she snags another man." Silas's unemotional face said he didn't care which.

"You're taking this very well."

"Did you expect me to be upset about it?" His eyes held a gleam of curiosity.

"I didn't know. The bond between a married couple…" She set down the pitcher on the porch rail and returned to her seat on the swing.

"It's deep. But so are the hurts."

They shared a comforting embrace with their eyes.

"Jada will always be a part of me in a way. But I've moved on now, too. And…I'm happy."

"You mean that?" She wondered if he was telling the truth or not. How could a man be happy in his situation? Even being content would seem like an impossible challenge.

"I'm doing the best I can to provide for the ones I love, and God is blessing me for it."

She didn't detect even a hint of wavering in his voice. Maybe he *was* telling the truth. "So what did you say to her?"

"I just gave her some vegetables and told her to eat better."

"She still doesn't eat meat?"

"No. Or hardly anything else for that matter."

Emily touched her bottom lip with her finger. "I've heard of people who didn't eat meat—all *Englishers*, of course, but never one who wouldn't drink milk or eat an egg or even toast. How does she live?"

Silas shook his head in a tight little fashion while looking at Emily's lips—her queue to stop teasing him involuntarily. "I always said she lived on air."

Emily removed her hand, twisting them both together in her lap, the heat rising to her cheeks at knowing Silas was having thoughts about her. Suddenly, Will bounded through the front door and took a flying leap off the porch.

Silas stood and frowned at his son, eyeing him sternly. "Did you take the scraps out like Miss Emily told you?"

Emily was glad he was trying to get them to mind him better. They were plenty old enough.

"Yes, Dad," he said with irritation in his exasperated voice.

Well, it was a start anyway.

"Thank you for supper, Emily, it was very good." He held his hand out to her formally, as he'd began doing at times. She shook his hand, letting hers linger in his only a second longer than she should have. God was helping them, for it was only by His wonderful grace she didn't jump right into his arms where he stood on the porch.

Chapter 7

For the last two weeks, Silas had been trying to teach his children a good work ethic. He'd given them both jobs to do around the farm and had lectured them at length about how God wanted them to respect their elders—and everyone else for that matter. He hoped they would take some of what they learned home with them to Jada. She was going to need their full cooperation to make it with a new baby coming.

But at last, they went home, and Silas was glad for some peace and quiet—and a relaxing supper with Emily as soon as his evening chores were done. Out at the barn, Silas caught a glimpse of the big mimosa stump he still hadn't managed to make anything out of yet. He'd spent his extra time lately re-doing the chores for the kids. He surveyed the mass of wood, wondering with his limited skills what could be done. Silas knew what he wanted to make with it, but it seemed impossible. A small, heart-shaped box with a lid that opened and closed. He wondered how hard it would be as his stomach growled.

Outside the barn, Silas heard something rustling in the tall weeds nearby. He scanned the perimeter, but brushed the thought aside when he saw nothing out of the ordinary. The little squirrels made lots of noise, and there were always plenty of them running around.

He washed up at the hydrant and headed to Emily's porch, hoping for some chocolate lava cake, stopping only to check the new strawberry bed Emily had planted over the summer. It would be two years before it would bear any strawberries, but the thought of more of Emily's strawberry shortcake had made it worth the effort.

Silas's children had been gone three days when Emily sat herself down, flat on her bottom to do some weeding in the garden. The ground that came up with the root clumps was cool to the touch, making Emily almost want to dig a hole for herself and lie in it. School would be starting next week and the thought of baking in a hot classroom the rest of August didn't appeal to her. She thought of the children, though, and a smile came on. Then she wondered if this would be the school year Leo Schwartz would finally decide to ask if he could court her. What would she say? Silas would tell her to go for it. But the more she thought about it, the more she began to think maybe she could be happy never marrying.

"You look deep in thought," Silas said as he passed by. He was headed through the yard toward the horse stalls.

"Keeps the mind young," she said as she watched him walk in front of her, his suspenders tight against his broad back.

Emily lowered her eyes and began pulling the weeds more aggressively. Of course she wanted to know what it was like to be married, sharing a bond with someone closer than any other relationship on the planet—but not with anyone but Silas.

"Emily," Silas said, calmly from a distance she

could barely hear. "Get to the house."

Emily looked up. Silas stood just beyond the compost pile, with a huge black bear approaching. She swallowed hard. This was the time of year they ate ferociously, trying to put on the weight they would need to last them all winter. They weren't usually aggressive with people—unless someone had been feeding them. This bear didn't stop as Silas stood with his arms in the air in an effort to make himself look bigger.

Emily jumped up, nearly tripping on the hem of her dress, her bare feet moving as fast as they would carry her as she raced to Silas's house. Out of breath she jerked open the screen door and ran inside. She grabbed a chair from the kitchen, running with it to the bedroom, hitting the doorframe twice before making it inside and to the shelf. She jumped up on it and groped for the gun. She leaped down and hovered over the bed with it, spinning the cylinder with soft clicks. All five rounds were there. Flipping the safety off, she raced outside, and in a gutsy move ran for the bear.

Silas had told Emily to get to the house. He hoped she had listened, but there was no way he was going to turn around to find out. This bear meant business. It stood not twenty feet from him, taking tentative steps forward, stopping only to stand on its hind legs in a dominant stance before dropping its massive body back to all fours again.

He tried to remember what he knew about confronting a bear. Running was out of the question. It only triggered their instinct to chase, and at speeds of up to thirty-five miles per hour, Silas didn't stand a chance. There was a tree not far from where Silas stood, but bears could climb one hundred feet up a tree in thirty seconds. He could play dead, but this time of year bears liked to eat dead things.

The scraps. Will had been taking them out for Emily. Silas could hardly believe it. If the bear ate him, it would be because he hadn't taught his kids to listen. Talk about a parenting mistake. The bear opened its mouth and roared, a deep sound from its gut, meant to cause fear in its opponent. It was working. *Please, God. Help me.*

Silas knew he was supposed to talk to the bear and not show fear. He thought of a Bible verse and fumbled for the words. "' F-for I the LORD thy God will hold thy right hand, saying unto thee, Fear not; I will help thee.'" The bear stopped advancing. If Silas had to, he'd preach a whole sermon to the bear. Silas took a step backward, "'The LORD is my rock, and my fortress, and my deliverer; my God, my strength, in whom I will trust; my buckler, and the horn of my salvation, and my high tower,'" he told the bear, taking a step back as he did. He raised his voice in defiance, "'Yea, though I walk through the valley of the shadow of death, I will fear no evil.'"

The bear was staring him down, but Silas believed in his heart that God would protect him. "'Thou preparest a table before me—'" The bear lunged into a charge. Silas darted out of the way, but the bear turned, paw-slapping him to the ground. Another fierce roar scared the wind out of Silas. With an open mouth, the bear's head came at him. Silas gouged at the bear's eye with his fingertips, his legs kicking at the bear wildly, but still, its ugly mouth was open, baring its teeth in a fierce snarl. The mouth came at his and Silas knew it could be the end. He closed his eyes hard.

A shot rang out, stopping his blood from flowing and making the bear hunker down on top of him. Then, with a quick leap, using Silas as a springboard, the bear fled. Another shot blasted his ears, and then another one. He rolled over stiffly, and with shaky knees he approached Emily, standing breathless with the gun still pointing to the field where the bear had sought refuge. He took the gun from her hands and she embraced him fully, her squeeze hurting his chest, though he wouldn't dare tell her.

Emily dissolved into a fit of tears in Silas's arms. He was alive. Never had she been so terrified in her life. Hands still shaking, she wanted to kick herself for not being able to hit the bear, even at close range. The first shot she'd fired into the field, knowing her aim wasn't good enough to try to stop a bear on top of Silas. But as it ran away, she became determined to kill it. Only by then her hands shook too hard to line up the sights. She would need to practice more.

"You saved my life," Silas said, with one arm around her back, holding her head close to his shoulder. The severity of the situation was beginning to sink in, and Emily didn't want to think of what she'd have done if Silas were killed or maimed. She clung to him tightly, thanking the Lord he was still in one piece. She felt Silas rest his chin on her *kapp* and then kiss the top of it.

She pulled her head back to stare up at him. "I'll never leave you, Silas." She watched the bump in his throat move as he swallowed, savoring the warmth of his body while she could. She pulled him close again, in a tight hug.

"We'd better get to the house."

She walked with him a little way with her arm still around his waist. Then he stopped, no doubt encouraging her to break their embrace. It would never do to be caught holding each other. Emily wished with all her heart there was a way for them to be together. She'd marry Silas in a heartbeat.

School started again, and Emily tried to busy herself the best she could, but thoughts of a lonely winter without long suppers on the porch with Silas assaulted her. The fall breeze through the open window reminded her that it would happen soon. Silas still talked of her settling down with a husband of her own, but how could Emily spend a lifetime without him? She sat at her desk, thankful for the end of the school day. Emily had her book bag loaded and on her shoulder, even before she called out, "Class dismissed."

Locking the door behind her, she walked toward her buggy, but Leo Schwartz caught her first.

"Beautiful day, isn't it?" he said with a friendly grin. He seemed genuinely happy—and interested. Was this the day he finally asked to call on her?

"*Ja*, it's fine weather."

"Almost makes me think of having a picnic." He was definitely hinting.

Emily couldn't let him ask her. There was no way she could say *ja*. She'd already promised her heart to Silas, even if he'd never be able to accept it. An achy sadness washed over her. "Norma Jo and I were just talking about picnics the other day. She said she keeps a basket of dishes all ready, in case someone wanted to go."

Norma Jo was the only other widow around Leo's age in Swan Creek Settlement. Everyone was always saying how wonderful it would be if the two of them got together. His smile faded. "Well, I'd best be gettin' on home now."

It hurt Emily to watch him go, but she knew he'd be hurt more if she went somewhere with him. She wasn't able to give her heart to another, and probably never would be.

Silas couldn't believe Emily had done such a thing. "Why? Leo's a really nice guy." He took a bite of beans and cornbread from the bowl Emily had given him only moments ago on her porch step. He watched her cheeks turn a shade darker.

"I'm too old to be going out courting. And a fool I'd be to try. Look what happened the last time with Nelson. He had the bishop all in our business."

She swung with her bowl in her hand like she knew everything, pointing at him with her spoon for emphasis. "And who knows if Leo is really over his wife yet. How uncomfortable would that be? What if he called me Gertrude by accident?"

She was making excuses. "Promise me you won't do that again." His voice was laced with anger, and she stopped swinging. "Promise me."

"I can't, and I won't," she muttered, though she peered into her bowl submissively.

Silas stood, setting his bowl on the porch rail. In two steps he was beside Emily and sat down with her on the swing. He took her hand in his, holding it to his chest. "You should have someone to care for you. Someone to love you and protect you. Someone that's not me." He held her hand up to his mouth, and with intertwined fingers, he kissed it. "Promise me."

"I can't, Silas." She was getting emotional again. He hated to see her cry. If her eyes pleaded with his he'd give in to whatever she wanted.

Not looking her way, he said, "I had my chance at love, and I failed. But it's not fair for you to not have that chance, too. If you love me, you'll promise me." He anxiously awaited her response, knowing in his heart he could never live with himself if he caused Emily to waste her life waiting for him. Finally, she nodded and his chest relaxed. But the knot in his stomach tightened at the thought.

Emily wished she'd never told Silas about Leo Schwartz. He'd made her promise to accept the next offer of courtship that came her way in an effort to get her married off. She knew Silas loved her, but that didn't matter. Or maybe that was what drove him to believe she should be married with children. Either way, she didn't like being told what to do.

Emily spent the next few months getting caught up on her reading at night, now that it was too cold to have supper on the porch. They'd tried for a while. Emily would sit cuddled up on the swing with a blanket, shivering. But finally, Silas had said no more. Now it was November and she had only occasional chats with Silas when their paths crossed in the yard. She hoped Christmas would come soon, and then hopes of an early spring could carry her into May.

The kitchen was filled with the aroma of pumpkin pie and organic pork roast from Silas's farm. He'd had an excellent year and brought home plenty of money from the sale of his livestock and enough meat was butchered for both Emily and Silas to eat until next fall. She covered his plate, careful not to let the pie get smashed beneath the plastic wrap and walked it over to Silas's door. After one knock she opened it and peeked in. "Silas?"

He appeared around the corner in an instant. "Suppertime already?" He received the plate, his eyes lingering on hers, making her long once again for the life that would never be possible. "I wish you could stay," his voice now much quieter than before.

"If you're lonely, maybe we could..."

"No. I'm sorry, Emily. I don't have the willpower tonight."

That was her queue to go. "I'll see you tomorrow, then."

"Good night."

She shut the door behind her, feeling strangely warmed by their short conversation. Back at home she ate her supper alone in the kitchen, remembering all the people who had sat at the table with her over the years. *Mawmie*, *Dawdie*, and the youngest of her siblings had eaten here with Emily many times. Sadness threatened to break her. She wanted to run back to Silas's kitchen and beg him to hold her, to put his strong hand on her head and tell her it would all be okay. Emily choked down her food, skipping dessert. She would turn in early tonight and hope tomorrow felt brighter.

As she stood, a knock sounded at the front door. She rushed to the window, peeking out. A police car sat in the driveway. With trembling hands, she opened the door a crack.

"I'm sorry to bother you, Mam. I'm looking for Silas Moreland?"

She heard Silas's voice from outside, "May I help you?"

The officer turned away from Emily and she opened the door fully, stepping outside, the freezing porch numbing her bare feet.

"Silas Moreland?"

"That's me."

"Sir, I regret to inform you there's been an accident. I was asked by a Jada Lawrence to notify you."

Emily covered her mouth with both hands.

"The kids?" Fear edged his voice.

"I'm afraid all three were injured. We don't yet know the extent. They were all taken to Springfield to the nearest hospital."

Silas didn't say a word.

Then the officer said, "Can I make any calls for you or give you a lift somewhere?"

Springing back to life, Silas said, "Yeah, thank you." His eyes shot over to Emily.

"I'll tell the others. We'll take care of everything. Go." But Emily knew that wasn't what he was communicating. He needed her to pray for Jada and the kids. And pray she would.

Chapter 8

Emily waited patiently for word from Silas. Two weeks had passed since she saw him last. Her brothers and a few other men took turns doing Silas's chores, going in and out when they had free time during the day. Luckily it was the time of year that Silas wasn't trying to grow anything, but the animals still needed to be fed each day and water would have to be broken, allowing them all a drink during the freezing cold weather.

It seemed Emily could never cook the right amount for one person, and finally decided to start planning for meals to be prepared every other day with leftovers in between. It was late, and she had already finished her supper alone, having changed into her nightgown and taken her hair down when she saw the headlights of a moving car outside. She ran to the window, cautiously looking out, but it was too dark to see anything.

A moment later, there was a rap at the kitchen door, causing her heart to stop. She hated being all alone on the place, but maybe Silas had hired a driver to send word. Emily peeked out the window to see the figure of a man, wide-shouldered with bulging arms. Could it be him?

"Emily," a voice called softly.

Silas!

She opened the door at once and allowed him to step inside. The light flickered in the lantern when she shut the door behind him. He was wearing a long-sleeve tee-shirt, a bit too tight in the arms, and denim jeans with tennis shoes.

"Look at you," she said, her heart sinking to her stomach at the sight of him. She touched his beard to make sure it was all still there. It was. He caught her wrist and pulled her hand down, letting it go gently.

"What happened?" she asked.

"It was a bad wreck. They were sideswiped by an SUV going way over the speed limit. But everyone's going to be okay. Jada broke a bone in her ankle, and Natasha has a broken arm. Will scared us all with a concussion, but they don't think there will be any permanent damage."

"The baby?"

He shook his head.

Emily pressed her lips together a moment. "Then you'll be coming home soon?"

"No. Jada doesn't have anyone else, and she still can't get around very well. I've got to help her with everything and get the kids to school each day." He pushed a long strand of her hair back behind her shoulder.

"Are you ever coming back?" She feared his answer.

"Yes. Of course. This is my home…if I still have a home after being away for months."

"We're taking care of the animals each day."

"And you?" His gaze was tender. "Who's taking care of you?"

Emily's eyes scanned the floor. "My brothers are helping out. You shouldn't worry about me. How are you?"

"I'm not well, Emily."

She motioned for him to sit at the table. She sat down next to him, feeling rather forward in her nightgown.

"The world is just how I left it. And it reminds me every day why I choose to live here, instead."

"Well, you certainly look different. I almost didn't let you in the door."

He looked down at his clothes. "That's why I'm here. I thought if I could get into my old clothes I might feel more like myself again. Jada and the kids are asleep, but the kids start back to school tomorrow, and it's so difficult being alone with her."

"You're tempted?" She could understand that, knowing now that Silas would only be with her again if they were remarried. They did share a deep bond.

"To kill her? Yes."

She laughed in relief. "Is she that bad?"

"I forgot how hard it was living with her, but it's much worse since she's in pain and can't do much for herself. And I have to help Natasha and Will, too. I just want to be home caring for the pigs, you know?"

"Well, I wish you were here, too."

"That's another thing. Talking to you...it grounds me. I need that in my day to make everything make sense."

She placed her hand on his. "Write to me."

"No, I couldn't chance someone finding it."

She touched her bottom lip with her fingertip of

her other hand. "There must be some way."

"Have you been collecting my mail?"

"*Ja.*"

"Good. I want you to read it. If there's anything pressing you can send it to me. And I'll write to you, but address it to myself. But you have to promise me you'll burn it as soon as it's read and never write back."

She smiled. "I promise."

He took her hands in his. "I don't want there to be anything they could use against you." Their eyes lingered together in a silent knowing.

"Your mail is on the table, along with your Bible."

"All right. Listen, I want you to take the gun and keep it near in case you need it."

"Are you sure?"

"You've already proven you can use it, and you never know what's going to happen around here. Just don't get trigger happy, okay? I see how nervous you get anytime someone comes to the door." Silas stood. "I'll try to drop in when I can and get my mail."

Emily's breathing became fast as she sensed his departure. She didn't know if she should, but she figured she would regret it if she didn't hug Silas before he left. Throwing her arms around his waist, she held him tight, and for a moment she felt the soft touch of his rough hand petting her hair.

A few days later, Emily found a letter addressed to Silas Moreland in his mailbox. The note inside had neither a sender nor receiver listed.

This was a particularly trying day for me. The Bible says to love your enemies, but I'm having difficulty just loving my family. All they do is watch television and look at their devices all day. When I mention the Bible, they crack up like I'm telling a joke. But it's not a joke. One day they may realize that too late.

I miss you and wish you could be here to talk me through it, but you probably have issues of your own with all the extra work.

Tell everyone thanks for me.

Emily may not be able to write Silas back, but now at least she knew how to pray for him. She hoped more letters would come and that they helped keep Silas grounded in his faith. Holding the letter in her hand, she read through it again, saying a prayer as she did. When she was done, she obediently threw it in the cookstove and watched it burn.

Silas dressed himself in plain clothes in the bathroom, the only privacy in the small apartment, and drove the kids to school. He did his best to drive slow, knowing the police wouldn't take kindly to a man with an expired driver's license—plain clothes or not. Natasha's arm was in a hard cast now, with her friends' names and other graffiti marked all over it. Not only did she think it was cool, but it made Will insanely jealous.

Silas stopped the car in front of the school and watched them walk into the building. He wondered how Natasha could handle a broken bone so much easier than Jada, but he supposed losing the baby had more to do with it than she let on. She'd cried the first few days, and after that had become snappy and distant, but she was slowly acting more like her usual stubborn self.

After driving back and grabbing yesterday's mail from the mailbox outside, Silas tiptoed inside, trying not to disturb Jada. She still slept a lot and needed to get up earlier, but this was the only peaceful time in Silas's whole day. He opened his Bible and read for half an hour, praying to the Lord to make him strong through this ordeal, and to bring healing to his family. Most of all, he prayed for Jada to stop blaming God for all her problems.

Taking out three bleached-white eggs from the carton, Silas broke them into the hot oil, their centers a pale yellow, so much different than the eggs he was used to eating. Emily had made his supper back home, but many times he would cook eggs for himself in the mornings, while Emily ran off to school.

Silas remembered her pretty face and the innocent way she had about her. Then he thought of the way he'd kissed her in her kitchen almost a year ago. He could tell from how her mouth moved, she had wanted to kiss him for some time. It was hot, but Emily had said all the right things, getting it stopped in time. He thanked God for her unwavering faith. She was right, it would have destroyed them both if he'd of gone any further. Oh, but he had wanted to, and at times, still did. He saw how easily the people around him laid their morals aside, putting them on and taking them off at will. Sometimes, it even made him envious.

He sat down on the side of Jada's bed with his crispy eggs, hoping the smell would rouse her. When that didn't work, he scratched loudly at the plate with the fork till her eyes split open.

"Did I wake you? Sorry, I was just checking in to see how you were."

"Liar," she said, sleepily.

"You're right, but really you need to get up. You'll sleep better tonight if you will." He could hear her tossing and turning half the night from the paper-thin walls that separated her bedroom and the living room, where Silas had slept on the couch.

"What is there to get up for?"

"Breakfast. I can make you some eggs." He knew she'd turn her nose up at eggs. In position now to call the shots, Silas had begun fixing whatever he could think of for supper, including meat for himself and the children. Jada, however, had been clinging to her vegan diet.

She rubbed her face with her hands and when she removed them, he could see pain squinting her eyes and making her forehead tense.

"Or, I could make you a fruit bowl."

She nodded, reaching for a bottle of pills on the side table.

Silas strode into the kitchen and washed and cut up a bowlful of grapes, apple, orange, and banana. He set it down on the coffee table before going back for

Jada. Silas caught a glimpse of her changing as he walked into the room. He stopped and turned his head the other way.

"Nothin' you haven't seen before," she said in a matter-of-fact way. She wasn't flirting, only being practical. "K."

Silas scooped her up into his arms, the only job in his new routine that made him feel like a man, and carried her carefully to the couch. She squeezed the muscle in his arm playfully as he set her down. "Been choppin' a lot of wood, I see."

He gave her a stern look as he handed her the bowl of fruit, but inside the compliment danced.

Next on his agenda was laundry and dishes. Silas started a load of wash, careful not to mix the colors and whites, as he did the first time he'd tried, turning all his socks a faint pink. He wondered if the *Ordnung* said anything about sock color. Then he scrubbed dishes from the night before. Afterward, he took the garbage out to the curb, swept and vacuumed the floors, and then sat down on the couch with Jada for a break.

She was engaged in some talk show about dysfunctional families, but quickly went to endless channel surfing when they began talking about pregnancy. He wanted to comfort her, but didn't know how. She had hardly said a word about the baby since the accident.

Silas's stomach growled. He thought of roast pork and pumpkin pie, the last home-cooked meal he'd had, wishing Emily was here to feed him. Knowing he was pathetic for even thinking it, he got up and trudged back to spoil a clean kitchen. He grabbed two frozen burritos from the freezer and popped them in the microwave for a few minutes. It would have to do. While they cooled, Silas asked Jada what she wanted for lunch.

"Could you make me some quinoa and chickpeas?"

Silas spent the next five minutes trying to figure out what quinoa was and how it was supposed to be fixed. He finally had to stop for an explanation and soon gave her a bowl of what looked like round rice and round beans. Then he sat down with her on the couch and ate his burritos.

Jada turned up the volume on the TV set. Her soaps were on, and there was no talking to her now. Everything had to wait; she wouldn't even answer the phone if it rang, not wanting to miss what happened next with Reba and Jack, her favorite soap opera couple.

Reba and Jack had fallen madly in lust last week when they were trapped in the basement during a freak storm. Now they wanted to be together all the time, only both of them were already married. Reba, to an old man who held her stake in the family's fortune, and Jack to a hospital office worker who had been in a coma for the last year. As disgusting and contrived as it sounded, it reminded Silas of himself and Emily. He left the rest of his burrito on his plate.

He picked up the stack of papers on the bar, along with a pen and the cordless phone. In Jada's room he made three phone calls, but still didn't manage to straighten out the insurance settlement with Jada's car. Now it was time to plan supper and go pick up the kids from school. But a knock at the door brought him to the window, where outside, two men stood in plain clothing. He opened the door, glad he'd worn his old clothes that day, and not a tee-shirt that showed the many tattoos he'd collected in his former life.

"Vie gatz," Silas said, taking in the sight of Bishop Amos and the preacher, John Miller.

"Vie gatz," they said, shaking hands with him.

Silas stepped outside the door, shutting it behind him. "Is everything all right?" he asked.

"We've come to ask you the same thing. How are Jada and the *chinda*?"

"They're getting better, thank you. I heard the men of the community were taking care of my farm and I want everyone to know how much I appreciate that."

"We're all glad to help, Silas. We were wondering if there was anything else you needed."

Silas felt his body relax a bit, knowing he wasn't being reprimanded for leaving. Silas stared at their long beards, coming down to the middle of their chests, wondering if his would ever be that long. "Yes, actually there is. Would you lay hands on me and pray that I can be strong living here?" Silas was close to unburdening his soul on them, and he hoped not to trouble them, but he knew the prayers of the righteous availeth much.

The two men glanced at each other. They removed their black felt hats and each placed a hand on Silas's shoulder and together they prayed.

"Thank you," Silas said when they placed their hats back on their heads. "I want to come home, but my family needs me."

"It's a difficult situation," the bishop said. "You must honor your responsibility, but you must also honor God."

"Right." Silas nodded.

The bishop glanced at the car in the driveway, a rental until the insurance settled, allowing Jada to buy a new one. Silas could see where this was going and decided to confess while he could. "I've been driving, but it's not my car. The kids have to go to school, and I do the shopping and take them to doctor's appointments." Surely they'd understand in this situation.

"And do you have a license?"

"No, sir," Silas said, unsure if that was a good thing or a bad one in the bishop's eyes.

"We'll send Wayne Stevens over to drive you."

"I couldn't afford that," Silas said. He had no idea how long he would be here and what he would find when he returned to his farm, making his financial situation unsure.

"Don't worry yourself with it. I'll see if I can get him here by tomorrow."

"Danki," Silas said, feeling relieved to have their approval. He would never understand why not driving was so important, but obviously it was if they were going to pay for a driver.

"We'll pray that God's will be done and that

good will come from this." John Miller shifted his weight from one leg to the other, giving Silas the impression the meeting was nearly over.

"Can we do anything else for you?" Bishop Amos asked.

"No, sir, you've done my heart good just coming here and praying with me. Thank you for that."

The two men tipped their hats. Their visit had encouraged Silas, more than they would probably ever know. He got into the car as soon as they left and hurried over to the school for Natasha and Will.

Long after the helpers had all gone home, Emily lay in Silas's bed, reading his latest letter addressed to himself.

Sometimes I wonder about the rules and if they were designed to help us, or just keep us busy. It's ironic how not having a car is supposed to make us less prideful, when now I'm struggling with the children who keep telling their friends they have their own personal driver, making all of them think they're some rich-kid celebrities or something. And Jada's much farther gone than I'd realized, not wanting to admit there's any God at all, much less one who loves her.

I'm struggling to do all the cooking, cleaning, shopping, and errands, all the while wondering how you do it with a smile on your face. I have to say, I'll never take another meal for granted. Your future husband had better not, either. He should cherish you for the treasure you are. And if he doesn't, bishop or no bishop, I'll punch him in the face.

Emily laughed out loud each time she read it. She wanted badly to keep it locked away somewhere, but she'd made a promise, and first thing in the morning, she'd need to burn it. "Oh, Silas, I miss you," she whispered to the letter, hoping he knew just how much.

Silas turned down the gravel driveway, turning off his headlights as he approached his house. He quietly clicked the car door shut, not wanting to disturb Emily's sleep. He'd been thinking of her lately, much more than he should, letting his mind fantasize about what he'd do to her if they were only allowed to marry. It was shameful, and he knew it. He blamed his behavior on the television shows he'd been watching with Jada to keep her from being lonely, but that was no excuse. He'd asked God to forgive him, but he knew it was still unwise to see her this late at night with no one around, especially since last time she was in her nightgown. So dainty and submissive, it was hard to control his primal urges when she grabbed him around the waist. Her sweet innocence was beautiful, and there'd be no greater sin than for him to spoil it.

He could slip in, get his mail from the table, and get back before anyone noticed he was gone. Turning the knob, he found the front door locked. Unusual, but luckily he'd brought the key. He shut the door behind him, and remembering the lay of the small house, he walked through the dark living room. Stopping midway, he thought he detected movement. His ears perked up to listen. A soft click, followed by a click-clack, the sound of a thumb taking a revolver off of safety and cocking it. "Emily?" he said, timidly.

"Silas?" A beam of light blinded him. He raised his hands up to shield himself from it. "Silas! It's you. You scared me to death!" Emily ran to him with the gun pointed down at the floor. He took the gun from her hands and let the hammer down easy before handing it back to her. "You were scared? I was the one on the wrong end of the barrel!"

"What are you doing here?" she asked.

He walked over to the kitchen table, the light from the flashlight guiding his way. "I just came to get my mail. What are you doing here?"

Emily followed him over and set the gun down on the table. "Your house is smaller and has less creepy sounds. I hope you don't mind."

Don't look at her. Silas caught a glimpse of Emily standing before him patiently in her long nightgown, her dark-red hair flowing down, way beyond her waist.

"You weren't going to come see me, were you?" Her voice was solid, and slightly accusing.

"I didn't want to bother you." But she was certainly bothering *him*. He prayed she didn't cling to him before he was able to get away. There would be no stopping him if she did.

"You're never a bother to me, Silas. Can I fix you something to eat?"

He avoided her gaze but caught the scent of honeysuckle as he shook his head. "No, thank you. I really have to get back. I just wanted to check in and get my mail."

"I understand."

He knew his words had hurt her, but she covered it well. "You shouldn't be here, Emily. What if someone finds you in my house. What would they think?"

"I've set your alarm clock so I can be gone before first light."

Didn't she know how serious this was? "Do you need me to check your house out for you before I go?"

"Nay," her voice cracked a little.

"I just don't want to see you get hurt." And if he found her in his bed, the hurt would be on both of them.

"I understand," she said again. Taking the flashlight with her, she headed for the kitchen door.

Was she leaving like that? She didn't even have shoes on. "It's freezing out there," he said to her back.

But Emily didn't answer, shutting the door behind her.

The next day, Silas had woken Jada as usual. She patted the big bed beside her for him to lie down, and exhausted as he was from no sleep, he complied. She carefully rolled herself to the side, her broken ankle resting on a pillow. "What is it, Ax?"

"Nothing," he said wearily. Certainly not anything Jada could help him with.

"Do you remember when Natasha was born?"

"Of course. I had to do the cooking and cleaning then, too."

"Did I ever say thanks?" Jada's hair made black ringlets on the white sheet.

"No."

"Well, thank you," she said.

"You're always going to be my family, Jada. Divorce hasn't changed that."

Jada blinked back tears. Silas reached his arm around her and was suddenly closer than he'd intended. Her warm body near his brought alive the dormant feelings from last night. He scooted closer and found his head moving toward her. Familiar lips met him warmly. He kissed her roughly, moving his hand down her body on the sheet. He'd done this many times before and had missed it. The soft curves reminded him of Emily's figure, but this was Jada—his wife—and she wanted him. He thought of Emily's innocence and what a contrast it was to Jada. There was nothing to be lost if he were to lie with Jada once more. How long had it been? He released her lips to catch a breath, her jet-black hair and brown eyes almost a shock to him. Had he expected to see someone else?

He pulled away slowly, feeling a dull pain mixed with confusion. "You're toying with my emotions again," he whispered.

"Grown-ups like to play, too," she said seductively, kissing him again, the way she used to when they were young and in love.

He let himself go a moment before shaking his head. "No. I can't." He stood up and rubbed his face and hair with his hands. "It's not right, Jada. You don't want me back, you just want someone to keep you from being bored." And he was only frustrated because he couldn't have Emily. "I meant it when I said you were family, and I'll take care of you as long as I need to, but we're not married anymore. You left."

Her eyes became hard. "I only left because you were buying into what those people were saying about ruling over women. It's insane how they treat their wives."

"Was I ever bad to you, Jada? Did I ever hit you or put you down?"

She hesitated. "No," she said lowly.

"No, I didn't. I'm not perfect, but I tried to be a good husband to you. And you left me like I was some piece of garbage. You threw me away. Do you know how that feels?" He clenched his fists, digging his fingernails into his palms. "Have you ever been rejected in your life? And now you're trying to do it to me again. Well, no thanks."

Silas stormed from the room, slamming the door behind him. Finding nowhere to go, he plopped himself down on the couch. The dishes still needed washed and Natasha needed her favorite shirts clean. She only had a few that were easy for her to take on and off with the bulky cast. He wanted to hit something, but there wasn't anything he could afford to replace. Wishing for the comfort of Emily's kitchen, he wondered what she would tell him to do. He'd almost forgotten how he'd left her last night. *She probably went home and cried herself to sleep.* It was wrong for her to love him. She needed a man of her own. But he'd been wrong for hurting her that way. Silas took out a pen and paper and began to write.

Emily was afraid to open the next letter that came, but she'd kept it a day already, and knew it needed to be destroyed. Pacing the school-room slowly as the children finished their projects, Emily fingered the letter in her dress pocket. No one could find it, as it could incriminate them both. Each time Emily thought of the letter made her hand jump to her pocket to make sure it was still there.

Silas had pushed her away when he'd visited last, and after much analyzing she knew why. He'd decided to take Jada back and felt guilty for seeing her. It was to be expected when a couple who had shared so much together lived in such close quarters. Of course Emily was jealous, but she knew that was sin. Not only to covet Jada's husband, but to not wish Silas the best. He was a man with needs that could only be met by his wife, and his only chance at that was making up with Jada. She figured that alone would be enough to make a man cranky, but there was more to it than that. He had avoided even looking at Emily. She knew that most of the time Silas struggled to keep his eyes off her. The man was hiding something. She wished she could tell him it was okay, that it was the right thing. He should be with his wife, there was no doubt about it. Emily just wished his wife wasn't Jada.

Jada was beginning to stand for ten minutes at a time on her healing ankle. She was still a long way from being independent, but Natasha's cast was already off, and Silas had taught her how to start the laundry and how to put the clothes from the dryer in a basket on the bed for Jada to sort. It wouldn't be long before Silas could leave and just drop by every few days to help out. Wayne Stevens had agreed to keep taking the kids to and from school each day, so the only thing left was for Jada to get around well enough to fend for herself while the kids were at school. Each day he tried to coax her to stand a little longer. Her attitude, the only thing really standing in her way.

"Come on, Jada, you can do it." Silas watched anxiously as she pushed the walker ahead a little before every step, looking like a feeble old woman, complete with the split tennis balls on the walker feet, allowing it to slide on the smooth linoleum floor.

"I'm doing the best I can, Ax. Just back off." Her temper had been flaring again ever since he'd refused to lie with her, bringing to light how sweet she had been before that, despite her pain.

"The offer still stands. You can come stay with me while you finish healing." He'd suggested it from the very beginning, but Jada had said she would never go back to the people and be shunned again.

"No thanks," she said, disgustedly. "I'll take my chances here." She stopped to rest, leaning her head downward over the walker.

Maybe he had pushed her too hard. "Why don't you sit down a minute?"

Her voice rose in agitation. "Because the couch is way over there!"

Silas lifted her arm and placed it over his shoulder and then picked her up in his arms. She felt even lighter than she had before. "You need to eat more," he said.

He set her down on the couch, helping her prop her foot up on a pillow on the coffee table and started for the kitchen.

"Silas?"

He stopped. It was the first time she had called him Silas in ages, grabbing his attention. "Where do you think she is?" The lines on her face told Silas who Jada was speaking of.

"She's in Heaven, Jada. All babies go to Heaven."

"How do you know?"

"The Bible says so."

He could tell by the look on her face that wasn't enough. "I know God is real."

"How? How can you know?"

He sat down, weighing his words carefully. He wanted desperately for her to believe in God like he did, but he knew it was easy to scare her away. "When you left me, not the last time, but the time before that, I held the gun to my head and pulled the trigger. I wasn't hallucinating, I wasn't drunk. And I know I pulled the trigger. But it wasn't time for me to go. The next thing I knew, I was waking up on the couch. And another time when I asked for a sign, I heard an angel singing in the window." At first, he'd thought it was Emily, but how had he heard her that clearly from way over in the garden? Silas sighed, hoping Jada didn't think he was an idiot. "But I never had anything like that happen to me until I let myself really believe it was possible. He's real, Jada. And He's holding your baby in His arms. One day you'll meet Him and He'll either say come on in or depart from me, I never knew you."

When she didn't answer, Silas left her there on the couch, knowing anything else he said would only push her further away. He hoped to have at least planted the seeds of faith in her mind, if not in her heart.

Chapter 9

Emily pulled the letter from Silas out of the mailbox. The other was still in her pocket, it's corners worn from carrying it. She supposed it was time to read them both. The sting of how Silas had left her last still burned, and she worried what they contained. More hurt? It didn't matter. She had to know. She pulled the old, worn-out one to read first.

You have every right to be angry with me. I'm sorry about what happened. It had nothing to do with you, or anything you said or did.

This relationship, or whatever you want to call it, isn't normal—we're not normal, and it gets to me at times. I find myself burning inside with impure thoughts that I can't contain. Your touch ignites a fire in me that I can't easily put out. Romans seven says, "I am carnal, sold under sin, and what I hate, that I do." I long to hold you, but know it will never be possible—not without betraying the God I promised to serve, and destroying us both. So what can I do? At home, I can get the ax and chop a tree to bits. But here, I have nothing, and everything around me is encouraging me in the wrong direction.

I wish there was someone who could help me make sense of all this, but they would probably tell me to move, and I'm afraid it's too late for that. The only hope I have is in finding you another.

Emily was in tears as she opened the newest letter.

I plan on coming home after the next round of doctor's appointments on Thursday. You can tell

everyone I should be able to do my own chores by
Friday morning at the latest. I can't wait to see you,
and I apologize for the last letter. I never meant to
sound so depressing and hope our friendship hasn't
suffered for anything stupid I've done while being away
so long. I'll see you soon.

Thursday? That was today. Emily hurried to the
house, wadding the letters into a ball and stuffing them
both in her dress pocket. It was difficult to crumble
Silas's heartfelt words, but it would make it easier for
her to throw them in the fire if they weren't so perfectly
folded. If she hurried, she could make supper for him
before he arrived.

From the kitchen window, Emily saw Wayne
Stevens shake Silas's hand before he drove away. Silas
was finally home for good, making Emily want to sing,
she was so happy. She ran outside and he told her all
about his plans to go back a few times a week to check
on his family at their apartment in town, but how he
wanted to sleep in his own bed awhile.

"I've got supper ready for you," Emily said,
noting the tired look on his face.

"I'm going to go check on all the livestock and
see what chores need done first, but thank you, Emily.
I'd appreciate that."

She knew he was right about the way they had

gotten closer since the incident in her kitchen almost a year ago. They needed to keep some distance between them or it would only make things that much more difficult. She went inside and prepared his plate, covering it with tin foil and placing it on the table in his house. She had kept the place clean the whole time he had been away, but now she made sure his wood stove burned hot to keep him warm this evening, and even filled the water reservoir to heat water in case he wanted to take a bath. With the bed made and the floor swept, she hurried back to her own house, deciding it would be up to Silas when he decided he wanted to visit again. She hoped that would make it easier for him, because marrying another and losing Silas as a friend was out of the question.

"I kissed her." Silas had his arms folded tightly across his chest, his black coat apparently not warm enough, by the looks of his shivering. It hadn't taken but a few weeks for things to go back to normal between Emily and Silas. Already he was telling her all his secrets again.

Emily sat on the porch swing with a thick blanket usually reserved for buggy rides. She was nearly rolled in it, with a hot brick from the fire at her feet for added warmth. Only her nose was cold, but she rubbed it with her warm hands once in awhile, making her fairly comfortable for sitting outside in January. His last statement had warmed her considerably. Was it jealousy or embarrassment at his forwardness?

Jealousy.

"Why are you telling me this?" Her voice was quiet, but high-pitched. She knew he had spent a lot of time with his ex-wife, but after his letters, she believed he didn't have feelings for her anymore, and if he did, she really didn't want to talk about it.

"I don't know. Maybe because I tell you everything."

Did she detect a hint of guilt? Emily had the sneaky suspicion that Silas wanted her to know all his wrongdoings, so he could better accept himself if only she did. "Well, she was your wife. What's wrong with that?" She hoped she hadn't betrayed her inner emotions with her voice.

"There's supposed to be something wrong with it. I'm in love with you."

Her heart jumped. Though it was implied, he'd never said it before. She pressed her lips together. Now he was going to ruin the moment by telling her to go find a husband.

"Well, what happened next?"

"We got in a big fight."

Emily let out the breath she was holding. This was all so confusing. "Do you want her back?"

He shook off her words. "What has that got to do with what I just said?"

"I don't know. I was just making sure."

"No, I don't." He was telling the truth. She was sure by his eyes—and because he wasn't afraid to tell her anything, it seemed.

"But I don't want you wasting your life here

with me."

"I'm not wasting my life. I've told you, I'm happy being single. I have my job and my house, and I have you as a friend." She meant it. She was as happy as a person could be in their situation.

"Then why did my bed smell like honeysuckle when I returned?" A piercing glare shot at Emily, sending her head downward.

"I told you, your house is less noisy at night."

He laughed wearily. "You're a horrible liar, Miss Emily."

She swallowed hard, waiting for what she knew was to come next.

He sighed, rubbing his hands together. "One of these days, I may not be able to handle this anymore. I may need to get away. And when that time comes, I don't want you to spend the rest of your life blaming me for your decisions."

"I would never do that, Silas. I promise." And what was this talk of leaving?

"I know you don't want to talk about it, but you're not getting any younger."

"Silas!" Did he think she was an old woman at twenty-six?

"You know what I meant. I have my kids, and I wouldn't take anything for them. Don't you want that chance?"

Of course she did, but not on the terms he was setting for her. "It's my life, Silas. You're not my *vater*."

"But I knew your father. And he'd never forgive me if I ruined your life."

"And he wouldn't forgive you for interfering with it, either. My life is where it's supposed to be. God has blessed me richly. I wouldn't have it any other way." Emily wondered if Silas would know she was lying, but when the truth involved losing him, she had no other choice.

Spring came, making talks on the porch much more pleasurable. Emily kept her distance from Silas, letting him come to her when he pleased, and trying not to be hurt when he backed away. And in everything, she made sure they kept themselves chaste and from the appearance of evil, always fearing that one day Silas may decide it was too difficult to love her from a distance, leaving her with no one.

"Organic corn seems to be the best crop for making money this season," Silas said. "And a field of strawberries, what do you think?"

"If you can wait for the strawberries to bear, I guess. Do you have buyers lined up already?"

Jada pulled into the drive and Silas stood, stretching his back before walking across the yard to greet her. The children stood close by their mother. Emily had watched them grow so much over the years. She'd seen it happen to her students at school as well, the process of *chinda* becoming adults. But it was a strange thing to see them standing there, talking as a family. Even as broken as they were, they shared a bond like no other. Emily knew what it was to be a daughter and a sister, but she would never know what it was to be a wife or *mueter*.

Silas swung the ax into the chunk of wood with all he had. With each swing, losing a little strength—and frustration. It seemed nothing was going right. He had a woman who loved him, and a wife that didn't. He slammed the ax into the stump, the two pieces of wood landing just beside it on both sides. It was the last two weeks of school and Natasha's teacher told Jada she may have to be held back. Now the weather was too wet to even plow the field.

Why, God? Why does life have to be so hard? Silas thought of all the families he knew: the Hiltys, the Lengachers, the Shetlers, and no telling how many families named Schwartz. All happy. Anytime you saw them they were laughing and smiling and yodeling while they did their chores. Why had their lives turned out so well, and Silas's so poorly? Hadn't he tried his best to do the will of the Lord? He set another piece of wood on the stump and swung the ax with all his might, sweat pouring off his forehead. Could he help it if he'd fallen in love with his best friend, Emily Graber? He'd displayed super-human strength in keeping his hands off her as long as he had. The Lord knew what he really wanted to do with her—but he hadn't. Didn't that count for anything? So many times he wanted to forget God and the rules and do as he pleased, taking Emily in his arms, and pressing his lips against her soft neck.

Silas shook his head. He set up another chunk of

wood and swung the ax. He wanted to think of her only as a friend. If he had never kissed her it would still be a possibility, but as it was, he knew they were more, eternally stranded in some strange place between friends and lovers. Maybe it was time to do the thing he'd been avoiding for years now. He swallowed hard. Could he handle it?

He set up another piece of wood, but when it came time to draw back the ax, he didn't have the strength. It was time to lay it down on the stump for God to deal with. Silas fell to his knees, knowing if he asked God for an answer, he'd need to accept it—even if he didn't like it. The thought made his guts roll, but the situation he had was too much to bear.

You know my problems, God—all of them. I lay them here for You today. Swing Your mighty ax and bust them to pieces. I'll do Your will. Please find the best solution for me and my family and for Emily. Bless her, God. Give her a good husband.

Silas felt the weight of his burdens lifting and wondered what it was God was going to do about them. Then, wiping his forehead with his sleeve, already wet-feeling from the humidity outside, he ambled to the barn. Inside, he spied the mimosa stump he had cut long ago. He was too tired to swing an ax, but maybe he could still whittle.

Made in the USA
Lexington, KY
11 September 2017